THOSE
- OF THE -
LIGHT

NICOLA CURRIE

Available from Black Hare Press in 2021

UNDERGROUND

WHISPERS IN THE DARK by K.B. ELIJAH
THE RETURN by GABRIELLA BALCOM
UNDERWORLD GAMES by JONATHAN D. STIFFY
PLACE OF CAVES by CHARLOTTE O'FARRELL
AFTER THE FALL by STEPHEN HERCZEG
BEYOND HUMAN by MATTHEW CLARKE
THE FALL OF PACIFICA by M. SYDNOR JR.
THE GATE TO THE UNDERWORLD by E.L. GILES
THOSE OF THE LIGHT by NICOLA CURRIE
TIME'S ABYSS by JAMES PYLES
UNDER GROUND by STEVEN STREETER
SWIRLING DARKNESS by SAM M. PHILLIPS

Black Hare Press
linktr.ee/blackharepress

THOSE OF THE LIGHT title is
Copyright © 2021 **NICOLA CURRIE**
First published in Australia in September 2021
by Black Hare Press

The author retains the copyright of the works
featured in this publication.

*All characters and events in this publication, other than those
clearly in the public domain, are fictitious and any resemblance
to real persons, living or dead, is purely coincidental.*

All rights reserved. No part of this production may be
reproduced, stored in a retrieval system, or transmitted, in any
form or by any means, electronic, mechanical, photocopying,
recording or otherwise, without the prior permission of the
publisher and copyright owner.

Edited by Jodi Christensen
Formatted by Ben Thomas
Cover design by Dawn Burdett

To Mark, for lots of love and light.

To Chonka, for always brightening the day.

Contents

Chapter One 11

Chapter Two 19

Chapter Three 51

Chapter Four 67

Chapter Five 85

Chapter Six 105

Chapter Seven 123

Chapter Eight 133

Chapter Nine 145

Chapter Ten 163

Chapter Eleven 191

Chapter Twelve 207

Chapter Thirteen 235

Chapter Fourteen 259

Nicola Currie 271

Black Hare Press 275

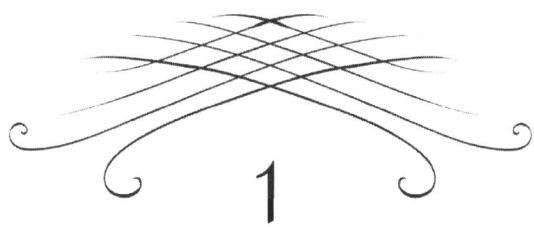

1

Frank had a wonderful life. He was lucky to reach the ripe old age of ninety with few regrets and so much love and light. If he lived his life again, he would change just one thing. If he could go back to the beginning, he would have courted Nora earlier. It had only taken him a few weeks to pluck up the courage. They went on to have a happy marriage for sixty-three years, but in the last two years, since she passed, as he had to learn to live without her, he thought about those nervous weeks a lot. They were a precious treasure they could have shared, lost instead to shy days of hesitation. He still remembered how pretty she looked, as he admired her from afar, still caught the scent of the flowers in her hair when the wind was kind and gentle, like it was the same wind that had blown then, that would still carry traces of the both of them when Frank too was gone.

"Not long now, darling," were the final words he spoke, as he fell asleep on the last night of his life, with his children, grandchildren, and great-grandchildren gathered around him. He didn't know if there was an afterlife or nothing more than ash, but he didn't care. Either way, he would be with his Nora again.

It was a lovely end, even as he felt the grip of his daughter's and son's hands become lighter and lighter, colder and colder, as though it were they that drifted away. But Frank knew he was leaving and that was okay. He felt at peace.

At least until three days later, when he awoke.

It was dark and stuffy, but a muffled cacophony of organ music, prayers, and tears sounded all around him. What was happening? He could feel his energy returning from somewhere deep inside. Was that all this was? A final burst of life? Would he soon succumb to frailty and unconsciousness once more? But he didn't feel weak or tired. He felt more awake than he had in years. For his whole life, maybe. But why?

He tried to move, but the walls were tight around him. He tried to sit up, but his head bounced against the ceiling, inches above his face. His hands searched, looking for a gap, a way out. That's when he realised. They weren't walls. His hands glided over smooth, polished wood.

It's a coffin.

"Now as we say our final farewells to Frank, and commit his body to the flame, let us all silently remember how much he touched so many of our lives."

"Oh heavens!" Frank knocked on the lid above. "Hello?"

New music played. "Blue Moon," the Billie Holiday version. That had been his and Nora's song.

No one could hear him over the sound of the syncopating piano, the riffing saxophone, as the knocks his family tapped their feet along to, even in their grief, became a macabre accompaniment to what appeared to be his imminent death by fire.

"Damn it!" he said, though not accustomed to using such language. Nora had frowned upon it. He knocked louder and began to scream. "Help me! I'm still alive in here!"

He heard a whirring underneath him as the coffin jolted backwards. He heard the swish of curtains closing and a metal door clanging shut.

He felt the rumble of the incinerator powering

up.

"No! NO!"

The sides of his coffin started to feel warm, to crackle.

"Oh bugger! Oh bollocks!"

The bottom of his coffin gave way and he fell. And fell. And fell.

"FUUUUUUUUCCCCCCCKKKKKKKK!"

At least he no longer burned. The walls around him were cold now, as though he was in a metal chute. He could feel a similar coolness beneath his back, too. He lay on some kind of platform, rushing downwards. The absence of fire only comforted him for a second, still falling, and at ferocious speed. His stomach lagged two feet above him, struggling to stay attached, like a balloon he was fighting to hold.

Is this death? Frank considered it as he fell for minutes, hours. Could he have even been falling for a day? Two? He lost all sense of time as his mind drifted in and out of consciousness. One moment he fell, terrified, with the rest of his body; the next he would be with Nora on their little bit of beach that came with the holiday cottage they bought for summer getaways. There he did not fall in darkness. There peaceful light shone: in the sparkle of the waves, in the glistening sands, in Nora's smiling hazel eyes.

He awoke from a sunlit dream of the breeze in Nora's chestnut hair. He was slowing. Inexplicably but unequivocally, he descended slower and slower, until he fell no faster than a head might fall back onto a pillow.

Suddenly, he stopped, the platform beneath him connecting with a dock as metallic arms reached up and locked it in place. He squinted as he opened his eyes, the light blindingly bright after so long in darkness it made him cry out in pain.

"Code red!" a female voice said. "We've got a

Dreamer!"

Rough hands grabbed him as he thrashed around and tried to cover his eyes. He saw nothing but a blur of faces as they pinned his arms.

"Wha... Wher..." He felt weak, unable to speak or think clearly. More hands grabbed him; frantic, crushing hands. *Is this hell?*

A shot of pain radiated up his lower arm and he drifted again. This time it wasn't gentle and the hands that held him were not his daughter's, his son's.

Yet, finally, it felt like the last part of him fell away. With the thought of a curse word too explicit to say aloud even if he had the strength, Frank slept and was at peace.

NICOLA CURRIE

2

Mrs Parson's blueberry jam, Frank thought as he awoke, sure he must still be dreaming. That's what they looked like, the eyes that stared down at him: two puddles of glistening blueberry jam.

Apart from her strange dark purple gaze, everything else about the young woman appeared human, even if she was a little on the pale side. Her black hair hung in one of those choppy bobs he'd seen on other youngsters—the lady could be no older than twenty-five—and she wore a black leather jacket over some kind of strappy black overall. As his surroundings came into focus, he noticed the corners of her mouth glimmering under the harsh hospital lighting. Both corners of her pursed lips were pierced with a small diamond stud. *Well, I never.* She looked like the punk types he'd usually cross the road to avoid, Frank decided, though he was sure she must be a nice girl, deep down. Her large, fascinating eyes were wide with concern.

"I'm impressed," the woman said, lifting each of his eyelids and looking inside, seeming to be satisfied no sign of damage affected his sight when he followed her finger without difficulty. "Most Dreamers never last the journey and those that do, wake up crazy." She took a step back. "You're not crazy, right?"

"Funnily enough, I've been asking myself the same question. I suppose it depends on where I think I am, and currently, my dear, that I do not know."

Frank sat up, rising with difficulty as he found himself encumbered by an IV drip and wires on his chest that connected to a monitor. It beeped relatively calmly given recent events. He could have been in any normal hospital room, apart from the lack of windows, the strange woman and an odd odour in the air. Hospitals usually smelled like rubber and disinfectant. This one smelled of soil, of mud, of stone. Of earth.

"That's understandable, given the circumstances. But I bet you have some theories. They'll all be wrong, of course. No one ever expects this, but you won't believe me, anyway. Give me your best guess. If you had to explain what happened to you, what would you say?"

His head felt a little heavy, a little hazy. How had he got here? There had been darkness…falling…no, before that. Music… Billie Holiday… A tiny room—wait, no, not a room, his…

"Oh God!" The monitor next to him picked up its pace. "This is Hell! I'm one of the fallen! And I was such a good Christian too: gave up my whisky for Lent, paid my tithes when I could, remained a faithful husband who always tore his gaze away from Mrs Parsons, even though she had a lot more than tasty jam going for her—"

"Easy, kid, easy," the purple-eyed woman said. "Does this look like Hell to you? You're pretty comfortable for someone who is eternally damned, wouldn't you say? And do you really think you'd have the privilege of meeting a person as cool as me? Who would that make me? Satan?"

Kid?

"Well, you do look like you would like that heavy metal racket…"

He didn't completely trust the young woman, but

his monitor calmed to a steadier beat as he realised the logic in what she said. He felt quite comfortable, despite the wires and monitors. Shifting in his bed, he checked himself for injury.

"Heavens!" Frank clutched his sheets closer to him. "I'm naked as the day I was born. What kind of funny business is this?"

The woman laughed but turned to face the other way. "Relax, kid, you're too young for me, anyway. Hurry up and get dressed. I've got places to be."

Too *young* for her? Now he'd heard it all.

He saw a small pile of clothes sitting on the end of his bed—blue overalls, white undershirt, underwear, socks, work boots—but hunkered under his blankets still. Something didn't feel right. He felt more than naked, he felt…changed somehow, a different version of himself. He sensed the answer right in front of him, but as though he glimpsed it from the corner of his eye, unable to focus, to see it for what it was.

"Can't quite put your finger on it, huh?" the woman said, her voice tinged with amusement.

At that indirect suggestion, he glanced at his fingers before turning his attention once again to his surroundings. The room was…

"What the—?" His focus snapped back to his hands. He held them up in front of his face, stunned, horrified, and fascinated in equal measure. The hands before him were strong and smooth, free of blemish or wrinkle. They were not his hands. At least…

They were not the hands of a ninety-year-old man.

Frank forgot his bashfulness as he stood and his sheets dropped to the floor. He examined every inch of his body. His torso was slim and muscular, his chest toned and defined. His legs were powerful, his knees and ankles free from the arthritis that had plagued him for the last two decades.

Noticing a mirror attached to the wall, he crossed the room and stood before it. He stared into it, as though looking through time.

He was barely a man, a mere boy in comparison to the fragile old-timer he had become. He looked just as he had at eighteen, baby-faced, his jaw line sharp and angular, his blue eyes clear and bright.

"But this is impossible. I'm dead. I must be dead." Could that be it, after all? Perhaps this was the end of his dreams as his brain cells fired their last, Frank's sense of time and reality distorted as they expired with a strange hallucination.

"Cute butt," the woman said.

Frank quickly covered his groin as he turned to find her purple eyes twinkling at him. "I... I was ninety. I was old."

"You're still ninety," she said. "You're just not old. Ninety isn't old at all. That's a lie you were told up there. I myself am one hundred and twenty-six."

Up there?

"Well, is that old?" He shuffled towards the bed and grabbed for the clothes as the woman rolled her eyes and threw up her hands in exasperation.

"Do I look bloody old to you? I've barely reached my physical peak."

"I…" Surprisingly, it wasn't entirely unpleasant to have an attractive (if odd) lady shout at him as he pulled on his pants, and he felt something stir that hadn't stirred in quite some time. Still, the whole situation confused him. "I…I'm Frank," he said. It was the only thing he knew to be true now. It was the only thing that made sense.

The purple-eyed woman seemed to soften, at least. "Nice to meet you, Frank. I'm Seph."

The woman was silent as he finished dressing and shook her head as he tried to ask further questions. She would say nothing until he followed.

"Get a move on. I've got places to be."

They passed along a long circular tunnel, perfectly round, as though it had been bored through rock. It reminded Frank of the London Underground. It had been years since he had been on it, but the memories his flashbacks carried of his East London childhood were crystal clear. He could still feel the wind that came hurtling from the Tube's black hole as he struggled for breath, crushed by the crowd of people rushing into Bethnal Green station for shelter during the Blitz. As the crush worsened, the tunnel had felt smaller and smaller, as though it was narrowing with his struggling airways. He hated being beneath ground level, avoiding underpasses, basements, and the lower levels of car parks as much as he could after that. It was why he hadn't liked the thought of being buried. Cremation meant he hadn't had to worry about the idea of getting trapped below. At least, that had been the plan.

As they walked, they passed other hospital rooms like his. Only these weren't comfortable nooks of recovery, instead filled with screams and commotion. In one, a deformed woman struggled with two orderlies, hissing and scratching at them as they tried to calm her. She was naked. The right half of her body was saggy and ancient while the left remained pert and young, as though she were some intergenerational hybrid, her frenzied behaviour suggesting a similar battle of two selves raged inside her mind.

In another, a man's old flesh had been almost entirely stripped away. What remained was painfully taut, with the skin a flaming pink as raw and shiny as a victim of horrendous burns. The man tried to move, but every tiny adjustment put a new section of his body in contact with the bed and he screamed anew.

When they continued, Frank jumped as something round hit the glass next to him, leaving a splat of red behind.

"Not again!" Seph grabbed a key from her pocket and locked the door of the reddened hospital room from the outside.

He turned to the window. The man inside seemed young, healthy, had dressed and was full of energy. But his mind… Frank could tell something was broken there, as his wide soulless eyes glinted manically, his lips painted into a huge bloody clown smile as he lifted the decapitated head of his unfortunate nurse and drank.

"Come on!" Seph said, pressing a button on the wall that sounded an alarm, set off a flashing amber light, and dropped a thick shutter down over the murder-soaked room. "What more of a reason do you need to get a move on?"

"You're just going to leave them there?"

"I've raised a security alert. The guards will already be on their way to take care of it."

"But what happened to him? To all of them?"

When they turned the corner into another corridor and the thick hospital doors slammed shut behind them, Seph slowed her pace and answered him.

"They're all Dreamers. Like I said, Dreamers either don't make it or wake up crazy. Transitioning from above to below isn't easy. The process of unaging alone is physically exhausting. You surface dwellers have been pumped full of so many aging chemicals over the decades, it takes every bit of energy you have to flush it out. If you haven't got enough strength to get rid of it, all sorts of things can go wrong, like the guy with the fucked-up skin or Frankentits. It's more efficient if the subject is asleep, to commit all their reserves to the change. A sedative is sprayed when a transitioner first enters the drop, but sometimes there's a fault and it doesn't get released. The long dark fall, the velocity of the descent and dehydration mean those left awake soon start to hallucinate, to go mad. That's why we call them Dreamers, though it isn't really dreaming at all."

"But I dreamed. And not bad ones, either. I dreamed of my wife and the good times."

Seph's eyebrows rose in surprise. "Interesting. I've been a Greeter for almost fifteen years now and I've never heard of a Dreamer who actually dreamed. At least not one who could remember it afterwards. Maybe the shock made your brain force your body into a semi-protective state of half-sleep. Good thing it did or maybe I'd have lost my head too. Come on, in here."

He followed Seph into an elevator. He started to question further but instead found himself dumbfounded by the number of buttons. They covered every inch of the lift, arranged in columns of five. There were over one thousand floors. They were on level six. Seph pressed the button for thirty-two.

As they descended, Seph yawned and stretched. "What?" she said, as Frank stared at her. "It's been a long day."

"Well, it's been a long death for me, and you still haven't explained why I've 'unaged', if that's what you call it, or why I am here."

"God, you surface dwellers can be slow. Too much time with your head in the clouds. It's simple. Everything you know about life is a lie. The human lifespan is five hundred years, not a hundred or so. That's just the rough number of maximum years those born up top are allowed up there. You've been fed a constant diet of aging drugs since birth, so you'd accept your days were done and come quietly, but it's not natural to age so quickly. It can be reversed, provided you can get it all out of your system. After your holiday above is over, you're down here with the rest of us, working off your debt."

Simple?

"What do you mean, my debt? I've never owed a penny to anyone, excepting the mortgage. What…"

Seph silenced Frank with an out-turned palm. "One thing that's true, whether you're above ground or under it, is that nothing in this world comes for free. You've had a privileged existence up there, a privilege many more can only dream of. Me? I've never seen the sky."

The elevator doors opened, and Frank followed Seph out. Instantly, his skin turned clammy, and his heart raced. They had exited onto a railway platform, with nothing but a dark circular tunnel to their left and right. Seph entered a code into a raised panel near the edge and scanned the metal bracelet on her wrist. A light on the display changed from red to green, and a rumbling sounded in the distance. A few moments later, a small driverless carriage chuntered along the track.

Seph stepped inside, but he hesitated, beads of sweat running down his face as he looked into the suffocating darkness of the tunnel, ready to swallow him whole.

"Where are we going?"

"I told you, this is your home now. I'm taking you to your living quarters. Get all the rest you can because the work here is nothing like you're used to. This is the real world, not the easy, breezy surface you know, full of light and air. This is real Earth, kid. Deep Earth. Get used to it. If you survive, you've got four hundred years here. Would you rather start with me leaving you on the platform, trapped until the guards get around to finding you?

THOSE OF THE LIGHT

You don't want to get on their radar, especially not this early on. They won't let you out of their sights and then you can wave even the little freedoms goodbye. No? Then get in, idiot."

It wasn't so much the threat of the guards, however sinister they sounded, that encouraged Frank to get on the train. He could think of nothing worse than a night spent on the platform alone, the round eye of each side of the tunnel watching him.

Seph remained silent for most of their journey. As absurd as it seemed for someone who lived in a place without natural light, she pulled a pair of sunglasses from her pocket and put them on. He figured she might be asleep at one point, as her head rested back against the window. The thought of escape crossed his mind, despite the fact he had no idea where he could go or how he could get there if he did.

"Don't even think about it," Seph said, without

turning in his direction, somehow sensing he was checking out the passcode panel on the carriage door. "Even if you had the code, the pad is also a biometric sensor. Your DNA is not authorised."

Monitoring bracelets. Passcodes. Biometric sensors.

On the surface, people had often complained that CCTV had become too intrusive. He'd once sent a strongly worded letter about it to the Parish Council because he was sure a neighbour's security camera pointed into his living room and he liked to walk around in his pants.

This was something else. Here, it seemed, you couldn't take a step without those in charge saying so.

With no other option but to hope he was heading somewhere safe, Frank passed the journey watching the sights as they whizzed past. At first there was only darkness, broken up occasionally by the blur of other station platforms. Sometimes, the carriage emerged into slightly wider spaces, caverns with fortifications built into the rock. There, the train would slow before meeting a barrier that blocked the track ahead. He had time to look around in one of these caverns and saw guards in brown uniforms swarming over a small rocky fortress.

Blinded once more as huge floodlights scanned over them, he understood Seph's use of shades. When the lights shut off and Frank blinked the blur from his eyes, he saw a guard on the platform raise his hand to signal another in the control room above, and the train moved on as the barrier opened.

They passed more checkpoints and larger fortresses too, teeming with guards. Barracks and operational headquarters, he assumed. Eventually, they became less frequent, and they saw huge graffitied tenement blocks instead, some hundreds of floors high, with little balconies and fire escapes that led all the way to the bottom, where streetlights lit up dilapidated basketball courts, small supermarkets, vandalised libraries.

Out of nowhere, Frank almost slipped from his seat as the train followed the track, turning downwards. It zigzagged lower for what felt like forever as it sickened his stomach, until it entered a huge cavern, bigger than any he had ever seen. A lake filled with luminescent buoys glistened at the bottom, revealing a dock lined with yachts and speedboats. Above, every two hundred metres or so, a tier of grand houses was hewn into the rock on each side of the cavern, all the mansions decorated with pillars, gargoyles, and intricate friezes. A spider's web of walkways connected in the middle at small circular statue parks, each with a towering fountain at its heart. The train passed discreetly through this richer neighbourhood. He watched people walk their dogs along the suspended pathways, waving goodbye to their friends as they left the centre for home. The day was ending softly here, as dainty coffee huts and tidy newsstands shut up shop. It must have been getting late, though he didn't understand how anyone could tell the time here.

When they next passed into a tunnel, only minutes passed before it emerged into a cavern once more. Except this was different. The previous neighbourhood had impressed him, but this was beyond anything he could imagine. He'd never felt so surprised and that was saying something for someone who, hours earlier, had believed he had woken up deceased.

Because this cavern didn't hold a neighbourhood. It held an entire city.

He had been to France once, but otherwise had never left Britain. He used to watch lots of travel shows though and the skyscrapered, giant billboarded, neon-lit metropolis before him reminded him of Times Square, downtown Tokyo, and the shining supertrees of Singapore all at once, and that was only from the outskirts.

"What *is* this place?"

Seph sighed. "Enough with the questions already. I can't explain the whole history of Earth and humanity to you in a single evening. Take a while to take it all in. You'll piece it together."

Frank tried to ask again, but Seph shook her head and looked away.

He was further disappointed when he realised the train would stop before it had quite entered the city. It rumbled to a halt in a shabby-looking suburb at the edge. It wasn't dissimilar to the tenement block communities they had passed through far above, albeit not as infinitely towering.

"You're lucky," Seph said. "The guy you'll be living with is a real sweetheart. At least, he is as long as you don't stare."

"Why would I stare?"

"Like I said. No more questions."

Seph tapped another code into the train door panel and re-scanned her bracelet. He followed her onto the platform, which exited directly into his new neighbourhood.

A row of high-rise flats with shops at their base lined each side of the cobbled pedestrian street. There were greasy-looking fast-food restaurants everywhere. He usually avoided junk like that, but his stomach rumbled as he tried to recall how long ago he had eaten. Not that they would help, anyway. It's not as though he had any money, and the last of the eateries closed as Frank and Seph passed by. Above, light shone from only a handful of windows. Despite the long slumber his journey from the surface had afforded him, Frank hoped his new home at least had a comfortable bed.

Seph led him into a grey block of flats, twenty floors high. The cheap strip lighting in the hallway flickered intermittently, casting a sickly green light over the damp-stained walls, the cigarette-burned carpet.

"Sorry, kid," she said. "Looks like the lift is busted again, and we gotta go all the way to the top."

The challenge intimidated him. He hadn't been able to climb a single flight of stairs for the last few years, reliant on one of those stairlifts he begrudgingly allowed his son to install. Twenty would do him in for real this time. But as he took the first few flights with ease, he felt the blood pumping in his veins, the warmth in his limbs, the air in his lungs, and it finally hit home; he was young. He had a chance to live his whole life over, after all. If only Nora…

Nora. His heart skipped a beat as it swelled with a hope he thought he would never feel again. What about his Nora?

"Are all deaths on the surface fake? Or are some real? What about—"

"Enough!" Seph scolded. "Jesus, most transitioners are just grateful to be alive and are eager to follow along like happy little sheep. You? You're a massive pain in my arse."

"But I need to know—"

Seph stopped on the step above him, turned and held a finger in his face.

"One. Ok? Let me get you settled and you get one more question. Deal?"

He nodded and followed her to the top. She walked to the end of the corridor and knocked on the last door. When the man behind it opened it, Frank forgot not to stare.

"Evening, Cragor."

"Always good to see you, Seph," the man said. "And what are you staring at?"

Cragor was the biggest human being he had ever seen. He looked like he had a body made from a stack of boulders, his tank top revealing mountainous arms covered in rough, grey-toned skin. His wide shoulders and thick neck held up a bald head so big it could smash through glass with the gentlest nod. He stared back at him, his clenched fists as big as cannonballs.

A sweetheart, Seph had said. If this was what the sweethearts of this world were like, then Frank was pretty certain he was as good as dead anyway. He felt that the safest response was to look at his feet and remain silent.

"Take it easy on him, Crag. He's had a rough ride. Something smells good. You pulling double shifts again?"

"You know I can't live off standard rations and the guards are coming down hard on the back-alley markets. I've cut my protein back by half and I still have to work a twenty-hour day to afford a beetle burger or an eel steak three times a week. But a man's got to eat." He glared at Frank. "And don't think you can help yourself or I'll be having Frank chops for dinner instead."

Sweetheart? Indeed.

"Let me see what I can do," Seph said. "A guy in the royal catering corps owes me a favour. In return, take good care of the kid. He's green as can be but show him the way of things and I'm sure he'll catch on quickly. Your Head Foreman's even promised a larger serving at lunch tomorrow, if you do a good job getting him up to speed in the resource squad."

Cragor didn't take his eyes off Frank, but his words were for Seph alone.

"Fine," he said. "You'd better bring him in."

Cragor looked even bigger inside the tiny confines of the apartment. It was a stark white room with more flickering greenish lighting, simply furnished, with a white counter with two short benches on each side serving as the only seating area. An oven, a small fridge, a sink, and a few cupboards lined the wall. There were three doors at the back. The one on the left was shut while the middle revealed a grimy bathroom with a mouldy looking shower. The third showed a simple room filled by two single beds, pushed together. A shelf with two books and a clock, and a rail with a few spare shirts and overalls, seemed to represent the entirety of Cragor's possessions.

"This is the room assigned to you," he said, opening the door on the left. The room had the same rail, where a couple of overalls and some grey jogger pyjamas, all wrapped in laundrette plastic, waited for Frank. The shelves were empty except for…

"Is that a hamster cage?"

"This is Tulip's room," Cragor said. In response to his voice, a fat fluffy Syrian hamster peeked out from a little wooden hut inside the cage. "Keep it down when you're in here. She's a light sleeper. Aren't you, darling?"

"I told you he was a sweetheart," Seph whispered.

Wonderful. In this strange new world Frank found himself in, he was last in the pecking order, behind a hamster. What a day it had been.

"Certainly, of course, no problem," Frank waffled, unsure how to make what seemed to him to be an entirely reasonable complaint. "Except, there doesn't appear to be a bed."

It was obvious what had happened. Their rooms were too small to comfortably house anything bigger than one single bed. Clearly, since he had been alone in the flat, Cragor had taken the opportunity to claim the only available spare.

"Of course there is," Cragor grumbled, a defiant expression on his face. He pulled the end of an old sheet that hung from the ceiling and tied it to one of the shelf supports at the other side of the room.

Frank had made himself a similar hammock from a bedsheet once when he was a kid and thought he wanted one. He had quickly learned that he didn't.

"There we are," Seph said before he could protest. "Night then, boys. I'll check on how Frank's doing later this week and I'll try to get that meat for you, Crag. Oh, I almost forgot." She reached into her pocket once more and removed a bracelet. It was similar to her own, but bright red. She grabbed Frank's hand and slapped it over his wrist. "Don't even attempt to take it off. The guards will know, and they take a shoot first, talk second approach, so be a good boy, yeah?"

Frank was exhausted and overwhelmed from

waking in hospital; from the deformed and homicidal patients; from the tunnel and the darkness; from the guards and their floodlights; from the tenement slums and the grand mansions; from the astonishing city; from his boulder-shaped flatmate; and from finding himself the guest in a hamster's bedroom. But he had to have answers and followed Seph to the door.

"Wait, you said I could ask one more question."

"I'm not sure what else you can ask that you wouldn't be better off seeing for yourself," she said tiredly. "But fine, fire away with your last question if it will make you happy."

Frank knew he was putting his heart on the line. Seph's answer would either revive it, as he had been revived, or break what little was left.

"I need you to tell me. Is my wife still alive?"

NICOLA CURRIE

3

As it turned out, Frank's hammock was surprisingly comfortable. Unfortunately, as it turned out, hamsters do not listen to reason when you ask them to be quiet.

He had barely drifted off, after Tulip had left her wheel and settled in the early hours of the morning, when Cragor shook him awake. It could more accurately be described as being attacked awake, a tenderness on his shoulder telling him a bruise would soon bloom there in the shape of Cragor's crushing fingers.

Frank didn't care about the lack of sleep, the rude awakening, or the unknown day ahead. He felt as light as air. While Seph couldn't say for sure either way, he was certain Nora lived. She would have come here when she 'died' up top, Seph said, and the risk of something going wrong, despite the dreamers he had seen, was low. Tough but level-headed were the words Seph had used when she described people who best survived here. Nora to a T. A teacher for her whole career, no one pushed her around. She was clever, could read a situation, and could play by whatever rules she must to make things work. Nothing could get the better of his Nora, he was sure, not even a place so far away from sunlight.

He would find her, knowing he would search for her for every one of his remaining four hundred and ten years, if that's what it took, while hoping he wouldn't have to spend a single day more without her.

He pulled on the same set of clothes as yesterday and went into the kitchen, where Cragor grunted at him to sit on a bench.

"Don't expect me to cook breakfast for you every morning, but as you're new…" Cragor clanged a meagre bowl of porridge in front of him. "Besides, you'll make me look bad if you're late."

"Thanks," Frank said, tucking in. While the drip in the hospital had given his body nourishment, he'd consumed no real food for quite some time. The small portion was enough to fill his shrunken belly for now, despite its chalkiness and slimy milk.

Cragor must have noticed a slight look of disgust on his face and laughed. "I've tried the milk you soft surface dwellers drink a couple of times, though it's an expensive delicacy down here. It is too creamy and sweet, like a drink for little girls. I prefer good old-fashioned deep earth caenosa milk and you'd better get used to it too. It's all someone of your rank is ever likely to be given. Besides, it will make you strong and resilient, like the worm it comes from."

Frank thought there was an important question he should ask, something Cragor suggested about his status. But it slipped away and buried itself, almost worm-like, into the jumble of confusion in his brain he was still trying to unpick, about his new world, his new life, as he instead suddenly felt rather sick.

"This…this is worm milk?" He struggled not to retch.

Cragor laughed. "You'll need a stronger belly than that here below, especially today. Your introductory work rotation is at the Barn."

"The Barn?" It didn't sound too terrifying. Frank had spent the first ten years of his career working on a farm, until the farm shop expanded into a small supermarket, and he'd been asked to manage it. But he had no idea how a farm would work beneath the surface. "What happens there?"

Cragor smirked as he put on his boots and walked out the door.

"Hurry up," he called from the hallway. "You're docked a meal for every five minutes you're late, and you won't have any meals you can afford to lose, surface dweller."

Frank followed him out the building and along the street, almost too distracted to notice the light was brighter than the evening before A huge floodlight shone down from high above the cavern, like an artificial sun creating artificial daylight. He would have marvelled at it longer, but he was too buried in thought, too worried. Why did Cragor keep calling him surface dweller in that disdainful tone, spitting out the word? And what did he mean by his rank? Is that why he was so unwelcoming?

Seph had made it clear two kinds of people lived here—those born on the surface, indebted when their blessed time above had passed, and those who had been born and raised in the deep underground. Yet it seemed both he and Cragor were of the same status, living and working together, both working class, both impoverished. And what did this mean for his Nora? Where was she? What was she?

The street was much busier than the night before and as they approached the train station, Frank's questions and distractions were replaced with the blank-headed, heart-rushing, chest-tightening feeling he recognised as his lifelong friend, panic. Hundreds of overalled workers gathered around the platform. Frank hesitated, but Cragor shoved him along, barging his way through the crowd and taking prime position. No one argued, clearly preferring to lose their place than mess with a man who stood two heads higher than the tallest of them.

It didn't stop the mob from swallowing up Frank, however, hot and dizzy now as panic swelled higher. He told himself he wasn't a little kid anymore, that he could stand on his own, push back against the crush. As a shove from behind knocked him forwards, towards a smiling, kindly looking guy, he put his hands up against the man's arms to control their unavoidable collision.

"Sorry about that." Frank smiled apologetically, remembering his manners despite his clammy anxiety.

The man's smile collapsed and his eyes narrowed. "Get your fucking surd hands off me."

Others fell silent and turned. He thought it was because of the no longer kindly man's overreaction, but no. They were looking at him. A few seemed sympathetic or embarrassed, making themselves small and gazing away. But for most of them, similarly hard expressions fell over their faces like masks. A collective hatred for Frank presided, that was clear, but he had no idea why. What had he done?

Cragor took a protective step towards him, and Frank thought perhaps he was a sweetheart after all, as, with final cutting glances, the crowd looked away. Moments later, a large string of carriages rumbled down the track and they flowed onboard with everyone else.

Even tighter in the train, Frank tried to find a spot where he wouldn't feel so claustrophobic, where he wouldn't give anyone further reason to dislike him by throwing up in the stuffiness, adding to the cologne of malodours already suffusing in the staling air.

He found a seat free in a corner and took it. He lowered his head towards his knees, closed his eyes, and pretended he was far, far away under an open sky. It helped a little, and he breathed easier.

THOSE OF THE LIGHT

"Get off that fucking chair, surd."

When he glanced up, he was once again the centre of negative attention, the temperature of the carriage shifted to an on-edge, anticipatory heat that goosebumped his skin and prickled his nerves.

He'd thought himself a man who could hold his own all his life, and he was a little ashamed when he found he had unconsciously turned to Cragor. But as Cragor came to him, Frank planted his feet and held himself in his chair. He had as much right to sit as any other passenger and with Cragor on his side, he'd be damned if he'd move for anybody.

To his surprise, Cragor's hand crushed his shoulder once more as he dragged him up.

"Stand over there," Cragor muttered, "and don't make trouble."

The matter sorted, the mob turned away. Frank hunkered in a corner, in confused and ostracised silence.

The journey was the longest forty minutes of his life, nothing but dark tunnels and festering animosity the whole way. Finally, the train slowed as it emerged into an immense space, almost as big as the cavern that held the vibrant city he'd glimpsed the night before.

Occupied by a large complex of warehouses, factories, and energy plants, the space bustled with industry. Huge water turbines that reminded him of Tulip's wheel spun in deep murky brown reservoirs. As he followed the others off the train, he stared down at the tumult the turbines created and knew he wasn't in Kansas anymore. It looked like a rushing river of shit and if that didn't represent his past few days, nothing did.

"What in God's name is a surd and why does everyone keep calling me that?" Frank asked Cragor, as he followed him towards one of the buildings.

"It means surface dweller," Cragor said, eyes forward, like he was ashamed to be seen with him. "Surds wear red monitoring bracelets. They're not used to things down here, so the guards keep an extra close eye on them to make sure they don't do anything stupid or cause any trouble. Everyone's calling you surd because you are one."

"But they say it like they hate me."

"That's because they *do* hate you. I hate you too, a little, even though you don't seem like too bad of a guy. But other surds—they come down here and act entitled. They complain about how crappy they have it now. They never recognise that they had things so good up there, while we've always been beneath them, working the same shifts they do when the powers that be call in their debts and claim them. Where was our childhood in the sun? Where was our childhood at all? I've been pulling shifts since I was a kid. I used to spend every working hour trying to imagine what grass looked like from the stories I had heard, and how the bunches of flowers I saw, when I was allowed to travel into the richer districts, could grow on it. I've seen photos since then, sure, but I still can't quite get my head around it."

As they reached a steel-framed building, they joined a queue in front of the entry turnstile, waiting as those ahead tapped their bracelets against a security panel and, permission granted, moved inside.

Frank quieted, not sure of the right thing to say, feeling both guilty and annoyed that he felt guilty. It wasn't his fault. He had done nothing wrong, but it was true. He supposed he hadn't appreciated how wonderful the outside world was and could not imagine what it must feel like to have never seen it. He never would have seen the wind in Nora's hair, and that alone was enough to make his heartache. The grey-skinned, grumbling people around him seemed to carry that heartache as part of their identity, as though clothed in a hopelessness that fit them as becomingly as their overalls.

Frank thought of the others on the train who had tried to blend in, to make themselves small and recalled a flash of red on their wrists too. If he had any chance of finding Nora, he needed to figure out how to navigate a world where everyone was against people like him.

"So, no complaining," Cragor continued as he reached the front of the queue and entered the turnstile. Frank followed and joined him at a long table covered in plastic gowns, goggles, and gloves. Cragor threw him a set. "Keep your head down, be respectful, and work hard. If you're lucky, no one will mess with you. You'll be under curfew at first, only able to travel between work and home, but eventually…"

"I can't do that," Frank said, his heart sinking. "I

need to find my wife."

"One step at a time, kid. You haven't even got through your first day yet. You'll have to get through quite a few more if you want any chance of ever tracking her. Survival, that's your objective for now. If the foremen think you're slacking off and no use to them, you'll get assigned to the Pit. You'll never see your wife again if that happens."

"What's the Pit?"

"The toughest work allocation there is, apparently, but nobody really knows. No one has ever come back. Seriously, you are going to want to put that protective gear on, so get a move on before our section foreman makes you handle the Squirm with your bare hands. It's 6:28. We've got two minutes and I'm not losing my lunch for anybody."

Handle the what?

"Fine, fine," Frank said, pulling the gown over his head "But you have to help me figure out a way to find my wife."

"Like I said, kid, you've gotta survive before you can thrive, but show the foremen what a good job I'm doing getting you in line, and I'll help you figure out how to get to your lady, okay?"

It was more than a fair trade, a shift for a friend who knew his way around here.

"Okay. I'll do whatever it takes."

"I'm glad you said that." Cragor led him to a wide doorway covered by a plastic strip curtain. "Brace yourself. You've never seen anything like this, surface dweller."

He followed Cragor through the plastic and gagged as he looked into the slimy, squirmy pens. Frank could taste his breakfast once more.

Cragor chuckled.

"Like I said, good old-fashioned deep-earth caenosa milk."

NICOLA CURRIE

4

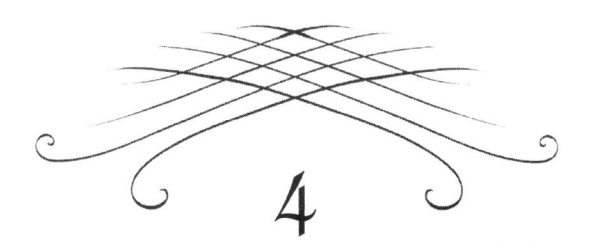

"Well, that was a new experience," Frank said six hours later. He washed his hands, feeling like they would never be clean again. The Barn was the district's largest milking facility, and Frank had learned it was his responsibility to spend the rest of his life providing for the people of that district. The young worms were twice as thick as the wide end of a baseball bat and had glands underneath a thin layer of skin that produced milk which could be worked along the length of their squirming bodies by hand, into a pail below.

Frank had experienced some things in his time, especially recently, but he never could have imagined himself wanking off a pen-full of four-foot worms. The stuff of nightmares, but he was surprised to find how adaptable he was, how it got easier and easier by the bucketful. He held up his end of the bargain and did a good enough job to earn Cragor a pat on the shoulder from the Head Foreman.

"Still," he continued, "whatever we're having for lunch, I hope it's not milk-based."

Cragor smiled and punched him on the arm in what Frank thought was supposed to be a friendly way. Frank was grateful to have a friend, despite the agony.

"I like you," Cragor said. "You don't bitch. You've got a sense a humour instead. You're alright. But don't get your hopes up."

After forcing down a slimy cheese flan to placate his stomach, his hunger greater than his disgust, Frank sat quietly while Cragor finished eating. He had been given two servings of flan, which hardly seemed like a reward, but he appeared to be enjoying it so…

He took the opportunity to watch their Section Underforeman as he wandered amongst them, a kind of electrically charged pulse baton attached to his belt. He accidentally caught the man's gaze and snapped his eyes back to the table, not looking up again until he was sure he had passed by.

Perval moved like he wanted every bit of his power on display, though Cragor had said that underforemen were nothing but guard wannabees who hadn't made the cut. Guards needed to be all shadow, many moving amongst citizens incognito, adept at blending in. Perval was a peacock. He didn't walk, he strutted and swaggered, and his grey eyes glinted like the threat of raised swords, daring anyone to come for him.

When the Head Foreman had stood on the balcony above the muddy slime-filled pens where squirms of caenosa worms swam, and called out the names of the new joiners, Frank had seen the half-moment of shock that appeared on Perval's face as he heard Frank's name. He'd also seen the smug grimace of pleasure that replaced it. Frank only wished he knew what it meant.

Cragor had noticed it too. "It seems Perval doesn't like the look of you, kid. He's an arsehole, but he's not much to worry about. The Head Foreman's not a bad guy and stops his men from overstepping most of the time. Make sure Perval doesn't get you on your own and you'll be fine."

Heeding Cragor's advice, he waited until Perval had left the room before he walked over to the display board. It had caught his interest when he entered the break area. He read the first flier.

Information for Surd Newcomers

The State of Sub-Europa hopes you enjoyed your furlough above ground. As you should now be aware, your existence on the surface was made possible by the efforts of your fellow citizens underground, as they tirelessly manufactured oil and natural gas for the use of surd communities, as they medicated surd water and crops to ensure optimum life perception management, and as they closed themselves off below so surds could live openly above.

In so doing, the citizens of Sub-Europa and the Under Earth International Government (UEIG) have met the requirements of the ISO War Cessation Pact. As per Section 22.6 of the pact, all surd citizens must complete a period of service within their designated Sub-state once their allotted time on the surface has been completed, lasting until their death.

Queen Gaeatrix, majestic leader of the State of Sub-Europa, welcomes you into her service. Her Highness hopes you enjoyed your time above and is confident you will be unquestioning and unwavering in your efforts to support the society that has forever supported you.

At least this world did something properly. He had always been a fan of the Queen up top, so if this Gaeatrix was anything like her, he'd sing whatever anthem was sung to her gladly. But the rest of it was nonsense. UEIG? ISO War Cessation Pact? He'd never heard of them. Not the first to have such questions, the next poster explained further.

From Above to Below: Common FAQs
1. What is the ISO War Cessation Pact and how

come I've never heard of it? *The Pact ended the International Surface Occupation War of the ninth millennium. It stipulated that the descendants of surviving Light Seekers would be allowed to begin their life on the surface of the Earth on the condition that they later join and serve their designated State below, in recognition of this generous concession granted by the UEIG. The agreement of this pact resolved the conflict and brought the Light Seeker Rebellion to an end. To prevent surds reigniting similar rebellions, the specifics of the Pact were not to be commonly communicated to subsequent generations of surds.*

2. What was the Light Seeker Rebellion (aka The International Surface Occupation War)? *Many millennia ago, mankind still dwelled exclusively on the Earth's surface. As a result of the development of advanced consumerism, the explosion of populations and vastly increased environmental* *threats, life on the surface became dangerous and unsustainable. The ingenious forefathers and mothers of what would become the UEIG established and developed communities beneath the Earth's surface, ensuring the survival of humanity. Unhappily, rebel groups, known collectively as the Light Seeker Rebels (LSR), selfishly prioritised their own wants and would not comply with the UEIG expert advice to seek shelter below. Instead, they waged war against the UEIG to ensure their descendants could forever remain above, where, without further intervention, their populations would continue to grow uncontrollably, eventually desecrating the Earth beyond rescue. The concessions made in the ISO War Cessation Pact prevented this and allowed for the cordial trade of goods and services between the governments of above and below.*

3. Ninth Millennium? *As a surd, you will be used*

to a different system of chronology, further confused by the artificially low capabilities of current surface technologies. The growth of advanced consumer-led technologies greatly contributed to the depletion of Earth resources and the creation of critical environmental challenges. Section 22.9 of the Pact demanded that surd communities on the surface be restricted to resembling far earlier, less resource intensive times. The surface you are familiar with now reflects an ancient society of several centuries ago.

4. What if I don't like it here? *Your happiness is not required.*

"Get back to work!"

Frank jumped as Perval shouted in his ear, his hand resting on his baton as he turned to him.

Perval looked him up and down, assessing him with a smirk on his face.

"You ain't all that."

Dislike oozed off him like the smell of caenosa cheese flan and Frank knew he had made an enemy, though the reason eluded him. He turned and headed back to the pens, feeling the underforeman's gaze follow him the whole way.

He spent the rest of his shift telling Cragor about Nora. He needed to share specifics, date of birth, date of surd death.

"I'm pulling another half-shift tonight and a friend of mine on nights has a brother who works in administration in the Department of Resource Allocation. If there's a surd called Nora matching the details you've given me, he can find out her work allocation and we can track her from there. Might be difficult to get authorisation to travel across the city unless we're lucky and she happens to live in our part of town, but we'll cross that bridge when we come to it. Maybe Seph can help with our monitoring bracelets, speak to her contacts to increase our security level…"

Despite his exhaustion and the ache in his arms, his shoulders, and the hunch of his neck, Frank was so happy he could cry.

"So, we could know as early as tomorrow? There can't be many Nora's that share her specific details and she's got to be listed for work allocation, hasn't she? All surds are, right?"

"Well, they are, unless…" Cragor turned his attention back to a particularly wriggly worm that, despite its energy, was no match for his grip.

"Unless what?" Frank said, sobered by Cragor's evasiveness. "Unless what?"

Cragor sighed. "There are two exceptions that would explain why a surd might not be on the list. Either they're dead or they've been bought out."

Frank couldn't consider the first of these explanations and he wasn't sure he liked the sound of the second.

"What do you mean, bought out?"

"If a surd has rich friends or admirers amongst the citizens (that's what we call non-surd underground natives), then one of those friends can offer to buy out the surd's work debt by making a generous donation to the government. It means they don't have to participate in mandated work service anymore. Usually this happens when a citizen takes a shine to a particular surd and wants them for a mistress or—"

"Excuse me? That's my wife you are talking about." He didn't fancy his chances, but Frank found himself balling up his fists and fronting up to Cragor, nonetheless. Mercifully, Cragor held up placating hands.

"Or they might have been able to skip the waitlist for a marriage license and—"

"That's hardly any better—"

"Fair enough," Cragor conceded. "If it's not that, then sometimes businesses in the city might take on those who are particularly talented."

"In what way? What kind of businesses?"

"I think they are what you surds call 'houses of ill repute.'"

"Are you trying to get me to break my knuckles on your face? I wish you wouldn't. I much prefer them unshattered."

At the end of the day shift, he left Cragor to work his extra hours and piled back on the train with the others travelling homeward. The train terminated at the station in their neighbourhood and he followed as the crowd emptied out. The caterpillar of carriages vanished down a service track as everybody else left the platform and dragged themselves back to their lodgings, heavy-footed and silent with weariness. Only Frank remained. He looked at the display board. Another train would arrive in a few minutes, headed into the city centre. The sensible thing was to wait until Cragor's contact could find Nora, but Frank couldn't go home, knowing she was out there somewhere. He would search all night if he had to.

A few new passengers joined him on the platform, and when the train arrived, they held up their braceleted wrists as they entered, the sensors in the door picking up and flashing from white to green as it accepted each one. With a deep breath, he followed.

The sensors in the door flashed again, but this time they were red, and accompanied by a loud siren.

"Unauthorised traveller. Please alight the train."

The bracelet on his wrist flashed a brighter red too, and he froze, his heart pounding.

"What the fuck are you doing, mate?" said a guy who looked not much older than he was. "Get off the train quick or the guards will come, and we'll all get shit." He took a step towards him and stomped his foot, as though scaring off a stray mongrel.

It worked. Frank snapped to his senses and ran out of the carriage and the station. By the time he reached the street and turned back, the train had started to move away.

He sighed. He'd never been the most patient man. What was one more day when he had been without her for years already? But as the train disappeared into the tunnel, he felt as though it carried all that he had lost with it, further and further away.

Still, Frank consoled himself, there would be answers tomorrow. There had to be. Nora had to be listed. All the alternatives were…

He tried not to think about that as he walked up and down the street in search of dinner. Cragor had shown him the button on his bracelet that displayed how many credits he earned when he tapped out at the end of his shift. 15 credits sounded like plenty, but as he wandered from fast-food outlet to fast-food outlet, he realised his choices were limited unless he wanted more flan, or dodgy porridge or any other worm-based products. After a while, he found an establishment that, perhaps because of the amount of grease covering its booths and tables, sold nuggets at a price he could afford.

As he waited for the server to bring him his order, he told himself things weren't so bad here. He and Nora would find a way to cope. He had a roof over his head. He had made a friend. They even sold chicken for dinner.

Frank was starving by the time his food arrived; he took a gigantic bite.

"Errgh!"

There was something very wrong with this chicken. The flesh was rubbery and tasted of a fishy sour cheese.

"Excuse me," he called to the server, trying not to vomit. "What are these?"

"The finest caenosa nuggets this side of town," the server said proudly.

Lovely...

Frank went home, his stomach and heart both aching for more.

NICOLA CURRIE

5

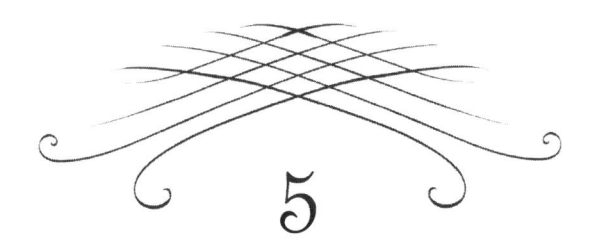

After another night of hamster-interrupted sleep, a repeat of the previous day's unpleasant breakfast, and an equally hostile morning commute, Frank's day worsened further when Cragor's contact told him it would take his brother a few weeks to track down where Nora was posted.

"I'm sorry," the contact, a pale thin slip of a man called Tilourik, said, arriving early for an extra afternoon shift. He had an eager smile but a body that fidgeted with anxious energy and a habit of looking over his shoulder. "My brother doesn't have access to the computerised central records, just the hard copy logs. He'll have to go through them manually."

"I really appreciate it," Frank said, despite his disappointment. "If there is anything I can do…"

"Nah, no worries," Tilourik said. "It's the least we can do for a mate of Cragor's. He's helped me out of a spot of bother with a few of the rougher members of our fine society. Unfortunately, they can tell I'm not much of a fighter and when rations are low…" He paused and glanced over his shoulder once more. "Put it this way, I'm not such an easy target when he's by my side. Anyway, I'll let you know as soon as I hear."

The shift passed much like the one the previous day except, every time Frank looked up from his work, he saw Perval watching him. At one point, as he fed manure to a new hatching mother worm,

THOSE OF THE LIGHT

huge, bulbous with eggs, and yet to be detoothed, a shove from behind almost sent him tumbling into the pen below, where the worm's fangs may well have been the last thing he saw.

"Watch where you're going," Perval said. "We wouldn't want anything happening to that pretty face of yours now, would we?"

When he'd recovered from his near near-death experience, Frank pondered over Perval's choice of wording, as he milked his last few worms. He felt he was right not to be flattered. It wasn't impossible that Perval had taken a shine to him and was using an extreme form of treating him mean to keep him keen, as his son had used to say until he gave him a good talking to. Except he could sense the dislike steaming off Perval every time he looked at him. He'd feel his neck sweat, and he'd turn and there he would be, eyes glowering. It was pure hatred. Mention of his 'pretty face' seemed odd. Almost like he was…jealous.

Cragor missed out on overtime, so when the day shift ended, Frank tried to talk to him about it as they headed back home, but as he began, Perval stepped onto their train. Luckily, he didn't seem to see them in the crowd and walked away, into another carriage.

"What's he doing here?" Frank said, half-worried Perval was following him home. "Why would a foreman visit our cruddy neighbourhood?"

"He's probably heading into the city and will switch trains in our borough. It's Friday. Most of the weekday underforemen go out drinking and whoring. We often get stuck with the old farts and the foreman apprentices at the weekend, too ancient or too green to be of any use, but at least they pretty much let us be. It's possible to trick them into giving you an extra portion at lunch too, if you're clever. I might have to risk it. I needed those hours. I'm hungry!"

So hungry, in fact, that when they returned to their flat and found Seph waiting with food, Cragor pulled her into his arms and half-squeezed her to death.

"Jesus!" she said when she could breathe again. "If that's the reaction I get when I bring you Grottofish and veg, I'm glad I couldn't get my hands on the ribeye."

"What do you do exactly, Seph?" Frank said, helping himself to a bit of carrot Cragor had already started chopping, and getting a concrete smack to the back of his hand with it. "I know you greet the newly unaged, but then what? Why do you have to come check in with me?"

"Charming." Seph gave him a mocking grin, the studs next to her lips glinting like sunken pools in the creases of her dimples. "I mean, I only had to sneak into the palace kitchens and get two great big smelly fish past a hundred armed soldiers without arousing suspicion, but you're right. I don't even deserve a hello, let alone a thank you."

"Forget miserable young Franky-pants," Cragor said, sweeping Seph off her feet and dancing her around the kitchen. Frank was surprised to hear her giggle like a schoolgirl, but he couldn't help but smile at the birdsong sound of it. As Cragor spun her back down, her hair fell away from her neck and for a brief second, he noticed the small tattoo hidden there. He didn't have time to see it clearly, but it looked like a half-circle with some letters beneath. He wondered what it meant.

"I love a woman who feeds me. My offer still stands, you know."

There was silence for a moment as Seph blushed and said nothing until Cragor kissed her on the cheek and returned to the stove.

"Besides," he continued, as he boiled vegetables.

"You know my view. I'd take every last morsel, every last credit, every last breath from the lot of them if I could. Royal scum."

Seph chuckled in reply. Cragor's back was turned to her, but Frank saw the fakeness in her laugh, the look in her purple eyes holding the shadow of something hidden, something untold. It disappeared like trains down twin tunnels.

"Sorry," Frank said. "I didn't mean to be ungrateful. I was wondering what the process is. Are you like a social worker then, helping people to adjust to life here? I thought you were a greeter, like you said, a kind of welcome party to get me established, but that was it. Not that it's not lovely to see you again, of course. I was just curious about what happens next."

"No, you're right, a greeter's job is basically no more than making sure their assignee wakes up, is healthy enough for work, is set up in their quarters, tagged with their bracelet, and introduced to their work mentor. The authorities aren't interested in getting more involved unless you act up or forget your place. I guess I'm here to see you as a friend, kid. It must have been the thought of that cute butt."

Frank took his turn to blush and did a grand job of it.

"Seriously, this is a social call. You're interesting."

As compliments went, 'interesting' was always an interesting one, he had found. Difficult to decode, more often than not it was sarcastic or dismissive. Other times, it was a statement of curiosity, the commenter keen to explore the subject's history or secrets. Only occasionally could it be taken at face value, a light-hearted comment that meant nothing more than an acknowledgement of the entertaining distraction provided by the subject's engaging personality.

Seph didn't appear to be the type to offer flattery casually, his gluteus maximus excepted, but not so uncaring she'd brush him aside, either. That left one option. She wanted something from him. The concentration in the deep purple wells of her eyes while she looked at him, considering, confirmed it.

But what did she want to know? What answers was she looking for in him?

"How are you finding things?" she asked, her eyes shallowing to a superficial sparkle. "I heard you've been slacking at the Barn. Not wise. The guards keep their distance only if you do your job. If they take you, which they will if you get too many complaints noted on your record, Squirm duty will feel like playschool."

Frank was flabbergasted. He'd never worked as hard. As he started to splutter a reply, Cragor answered for him, turning away from the stove with a frown.

"Who said he was a bad worker? In two days, he's more productive than most and he doesn't whinge. Do you think he'd still be living with me if he did? I'd have sent him packing to one of the fifty-bunk work dorms, like I did with the four before him."

Suddenly, he felt incredibly grateful for his hammock. And Tulip was a darling once you got over the noise and smell.

A look of concern washed over Seph's face. "That's odd. Has he been shooting his mouth off? Demanding to be taken back to the surface?"

"No," Cragor continued. "I've been helping him ask after his wife, but we've been discreet about it."

Frank tried to speak for himself, but Seph shushed him. He felt like a little boy, his parents deciding how bad he'd been. It was just another humiliation after all he had been through; he barely minded anymore. He'd left most of his pride at the bottom of his first bucket of worm milk.

"That's nothing," Seph agreed. "Most surds get a bit obsessed with the search for their surface spouse until they learn to let it go. The authorities value a little angst and heartbreak because the depression that follows shatters surds so completely it prevents resistance. There must be something else. You made any enemies, kid?"

"Of course not. My section underforeman hates me but—"

"Hates you? Underforemen are instructed to ensure they never get too friendly with their labourers, sure, but that breeds indifference, not hatred. What did you do?"

"I didn't do anything!" Frank said, more shrilly than he would have liked. "He said I had a pretty face, so I figured he was jealous."

Seph and Cragor stared at him silently for a moment. In perfect unison, they burst into laughter.

Rude.

"I don't think that's it, kid, but give me his details. I'll look into him and try to find out what his problem is."

"You'll *look into him*?" The more he got to know Seph, the more he understood she was not quite what she seemed. A worrying thought occurred to him. "Who are you really? In this world, I mean. You sound like a gangster or…"

Something clicked.

Cragor's status was barely better than a surd, like he'd got himself into trouble, into a debt he needed to pay back to society. And Frank had learned enough about work credits to know all the Barn overtime in the universe wouldn't keep a mountain of a man like him fed. And he'd nicked his bed.

Seph seemed to have her hands in a lot of pies. She had more travel clearance than anyone he had encountered. She could look into people. She had the skills to steal from a palace protected by soldiers.

"You're criminals," he said, as realisation dawned.

Cragor and Seph did not deny it but stared back silently. They didn't seem the slightest bit ashamed.

"Is that why you're a helper? Is that how you recruit people, because, if so, I'll tell you right now, I am not interested and would have no option but to report any signs of illegal activity to the necessary authorities. So, I suggest—"

His world tilted backwards as Seph grabbed him by the collar and shoved him onto the counter, pinning and glowering over him with surprising strength and fury.

"You suggest what?" she said. "Who are *you* to suggest anything? *You* don't know, with your childhood full of stars and sunsets. So what if we keep our eyes open, take what we need to help those who have nothing, trade whatever secrets we can to help each other survive? Who are the real criminals? What about the ones who just accept the shitty life everyone has down here unless they're lucky enough to be born into our corrupt elite, no matter how many others have to work and hunger? Aren't they the real criminals? Not the rest of us who try to fight for something better, fairer. Even if it is nothing more than a couple of stinking fish."

She huffed and shoved herself off him. A few seconds passed before he had the nerve to rise. When he did, Cragor smacked him back again with a light push to the face. Frank fell like he had collided with a brick wall.

"Stay down, idiot, if you'd prefer to be a pushover. I'll have your share of dinner, too, if you like. It's stolen property, after all. Ignore him, Seph," Cragor continued, placing a much gentler, calming hand on her shoulder, halting her agitated pace around the apartment. "He doesn't get it. How could he?"

Frank rose again, more tentatively this time.

"I'm...I'm sorry, ok? The last thing I want is to fall out with you. You're the only friends I've got. I've just never been the rebellious sort."

Seph still stared at him with eyes of purple flame but sighed and calmed a little.

"That's because you've never had to be."

Cragor finished cooking dinner and they ate it in silence. It was the best thing he had eaten in longer than he could remember, but he couldn't enjoy it. He felt he was right and wrong at the same time, as he often had on the rare occasions he and Nora had had a difference of opinion. It was true that life here seemed unfair, with most people working like slaves, tending to monsters, while a precious few walked their pooches around their mansioned streets and fountained parks. He supposed that was true up above in its own way, but it was starker here, more extreme. Seph was right. Even the unluckiest of those above had the stars, the sun, the air. It made a difference. It mattered. It meant there was some part of them—the part that could gaze, wonder, breathe—that couldn't be taken. That was their own. Ever free.

Frank thought again of the grey-skinned, grumbling workers on the train and in the Barn, and realised that was why they hated him, however unkind it might be.

And the level of monitoring, the invisible yet omnipresent guards, chilled Frank to his bones. But what could he do but accept how things were? He couldn't afford to take any risks of trouble, or he might never find Nora. That was all he could care about.

"Have you really never bent the rules or rebelled?" Seph said when she had calmed, looking only slightly sorry for her outburst. "Not even a little?"

He had forgotten to take back a library book once, and by the time he noticed the fine was astronomical, so he snuck the book onto the shelf when the librarian turned away, knowing he could never return. He had guilty nightmares sometimes, where he was chased naked through an endless aisle of books, the librarian's tuts and shushes getting louder and louder, as wild loose pages nipped his bare behind with vicious paper cuts. But he didn't feel like being laughed at again.

"No," he fibbed. "Nothing of the sort."

"What about Nora?" Seph asked. "Would you do it for her? Because if not, good luck getting remarried to her, even if you do find her. It will take you at least two hundred and fifty years to save for a license if you take every bit of overtime you can, and then there's no guarantee. And without that, unless you are assigned to the same district, your travel clearance won't match, so you probably won't share any permitted travel zones. The best you can hope for then is ending up as pen pals and more mail gets lost in the vast dark freight tunnels than ever makes it through."

As Cragor and Seph chatted and flirted over the promise of future purloined meals, Frank washed the dishes and thought over what Seph had said. By the time she got up to leave, his priorities were clear.

"I'd do anything," he said, as Seph paused in the doorway to listen. "I'd do anything to get Nora back, for good, like we used to be, no matter how many rules I had to break, no matter how many tunnels I had to dig to get out of this place."

At those last words, a spark of a look passed between Seph and Cragor.

"So, if there's any…er…jobs you need me to assist with, in exchange for helping me get my Nora, then just say. Although…" He had already asked, but he still didn't understand.

"Spit it out, kid. We've cleared the air, we're on the same page. No further need for countertop wrestling."

It didn't make sense. Seph could ask anyone she met as a helper. Surds who had been actual criminals, surds far more cunning and dangerous than him.

"I don't get it. Why me?"

She smiled, and the sparkle returned to her eyes.

"I told you. You're interesting. Dreamer."

With a stealthy peck on the cheek for Cragor and a deep-eyed smile for Frank, Seph left without another word.

Cragor chuckled. "That's Seph for you, a walking enigma. Don't worry about her. She knows what she's doing, and you can see she's a good sort. I'm still trying to work her out myself most of the time. That's the way she is."

Frank watched her disappear down the corridor, fascinated yet uncertain. More than anything, he wondered where Seph was going. Where she really belonged.

6

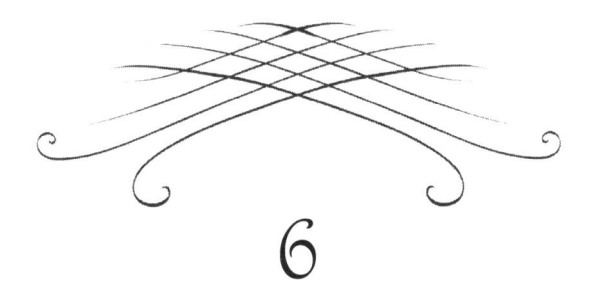

That was the thing about Cragor, Frank found himself realising. He really *was* a sweetheart. He could crush a man, sure, but he couldn't stay mad. The next morning, when they woke, it was like nothing had happened the night before. He made breakfast like he said he wouldn't and this time, when someone told Frank to move seats on the train, Cragor clicked his knuckles and they backed off. Cragor was his buddy and Frank knew he had done little to deserve it.

Most people seemed to see him the same way, too. They respected him, that was clear, but it wasn't because he was so intimidating. They liked him too. Nods, waves, and high-fives greeted him whenever he entered the milking pens.

So, when Frank noticed the turning backs, the grimacing mouths, the hostile eyes that stared at them as they arrived that morning, he knew something was wrong.

They didn't have a chance to herd their first worms before a bald little man, barely bigger than one of Cragor's legs, came up to them. He gave Cragor what was supposed to be an aggressive shove, but it had as much impact as an ant pushing a mountain. Cragor hardly reacted, turning around wafting his hand, as though brushing away a pest.

"What the fuck have you done to Tilourik?" the little man spat, head shining with furious sweat. "What shit have you got him into?"

Panic rose to a ticking heartbeat in Frank's throat.

"I'm his bunkmate," the man continued. "And he never made it home this morning. I thought he might have got lucky and caught a triple shift, but the guys here told me one of the night foremen pulled him off the floor a few hours before dawn. He hasn't been seen since, but some scary murder-eyed motherfucker and his guards have."

If not for his concern for Tilourik's whereabouts and the guilt sprouting inside him like a weed, Frank would have asked what the man meant by 'murder-eyed', but as he followed the sound of laughter, he saw for himself.

Perval stood with a group of guards on the balcony above, thanking and welcoming them with excited shakes of hand and keen pats of shoulder. They smirked at him like he was an irritating little brother, whispering to each other snidely as he moved between them. On a step above them all stood a pale man with ice blond hair, his expression difficult to read if not for his thin, sharp smile. His eyes were entirely red and looked more like pools of blood collected in his skull. Perval bowed before him.

"Damn!" Cragor said. "That's Caligo."

"Fucking Caligo?" The bald man whispered, afraid of attracting attention. "If he's crawled out from the shadows of the Pit to visit here, then not only is Tilourik a dead man, some shit is going down today. Since when has Caligo himself attended a simple Pit arrest? If Tilourik and his brother have been caught snooping, then the guards would come for them, sure, but Caligo? This is a round-up."

Others had noticed too, Frank realised. The Barn was unusually quiet, as every worker there lowered their eyes to the ground. They all grabbed worms

THOSE OF THE LIGHT

and, keeping their questions to a murmur, worked as diligently and invisibly as they could.

"Who's Caligo?" he whispered.

"The so-called Dark Prince," Cragor growled. "The Queen's son, and Commander of the Pit. The Pit is our continent's mass oil reservoir. It fills a cavern as wide and deep as an ocean, they say. Anyone taken by the guards could end up working in one of the oil production mills that fill up the Pit. It's said to be as hot as hell itself, and the work is brutal. Though I'm not sure where the stories come from. No one ever makes it back."

The bald man turned to Frank and spat out his words, forgetting to whisper. "And you, you little prick, your mischief with Tilourik has brought them here so they can draft the rest of us. When they're low on workers, they conscript new ones from underperforming barns and factories. They might take any of us. And it's your fucking fault!"

"Keep your voice down," Cragor said through gritted teeth. "We're not underperforming, though. It doesn't make sense for him to choose here. There must be another reason."

Frank glanced up. He saw Caligo slap Perval affectionately but patronisingly on the shoulder, as though acknowledging an old subordinate, and knew Cragor was right. There was another reason.

Perval glared at him with a smug victory gleaming in his eyes and Frank understood. It *was* because of him, but not in the way Tilourik's friend thought. The inexplicable hatred Perval had for him meant he would send dozens of innocents to the Pit, as long as Frank would share their fate.

As they all continued with their work, the guards wandered amongst them, assessing the best workers. He could feel the target on his back though he wasn't the strongest or fittest. He knew, somehow, Perval would make it happen.

Sure enough, an hour in, Perval ordered him and the little bald guy to work together on the walkways above the mother pens, feeding.

"It looked like you two could use a lesson in teamwork," he sneered. "I'll have no schoolgirl bitching and bickering in my squad. Get to it!"

Frank could sense it in the hairs on his neck. Perval was playing some sort of game. He didn't let on, but he kept the corner of his eye on him as they worked along the pens.

Perval didn't make his move until they had reached the furthest pen. It turned around a corner, into a semi-blind spot for the Head Foreman's balcony above. In the pen below was the angriest, fattest, most shark-toothed mother of a caenosa worm Frank had ever seen.

With a smile so smug Frank wouldn't have been surprised if Perval had started touching himself, the underforeman ran towards him, arms outstretched.

Frank anchored on to one of the balcony support poles, certain Perval was going to push him over, then heard a scream beside him.

He watched as the little bald man spun a three-sixty in the air, landing feet first into the gaping mouth of the ferocious mother worm below. He slotted in seamlessly. His eyebrows barely had a chance to register his surprise as the corrugated teeth clenched around his neck, his shocked face flying upwards as his head pinged off like popcorn.

"What have you done?" Perval shouted, projecting for all to hear. Before Frank could protest, cramping agony surged through him as Perval's electric baton sunk him to his knees.

"What on earth is going on?" Caligo said once he and his guards had moved towards the commotion. He looked over the edge. "Oh dear."

"These two were the ones arguing earlier," Perval said, acting up a storm in the role of agitated underforeman thwarted by his violent subordinate. "He attacked so suddenly, the other one fell before I could do anything."

"Oh yes, I think I saw a little squabble going on below at some point," Caligo said, almost bored. His red eyes turned to Frank. They were intense and terrifying up close, rimmed with a thick, dark black. "Now, is that really the most gentlemanly way to settle a disagreement? Though I suppose it's not much of a waste, tiny thing that he is. Well, was."

His guards chuckled. Perval joined in with his own fake guffaw a half beat later, though it was badly timed, and too earnest. Caligo seemed to breathe it in like oxygen, accepting it as his due, as only one used to endless sycophancy could.

"The cheek of him," Perval said. "Breaking the law so savagely in your presence. On the other hand, at least it saves your guards a separate trip here. He'll be coming with you now, I would imagine, though he is far from the pick of the litter."

"I...I..." Frank tried to explain, to stand, but his body still quivered and quaked. This couldn't be his fate; to be taken into some shadowy hell on a stranger's whim, without ever knowing why.

"Yes, he's quite pathetic," Caligo said, sparing him one more moment's glance. "Still, we can...make use of him. Take him."

As two guards dragged him down the stairs, each step battering his knees, Frank moved his lips to say something, anything, in his own defence. Nothing came out but drool.

The guards dumped him on the floor of the break area, at the feet of the other drafted men.

"Is this all of them?" Caligo asked the Head Foreman.

"Not quite," the Head Foreman said, clipboard in hand, ticking off the name of each chosen worker. "Your men are gathering the last half dozen now.

Sorry, your highness, not him."

If Frank wasn't already prostrate, he would have collapsed with relief when he raised his head to find himself at the end of the Head Foreman's pointed pencil.

"His debt's been bought out, I'm afraid. First thing this morning. We've been holding him while arrangements for his transfer are made."

The smugness tumbled from Perval's face like a bald man falling into a caenosa pen. "Surely, it doesn't make a difference, boss, given what he did? That's a crime no matter who he belongs to."

"Usually, yes, except when—"

"Except when he's the property of royalty," Caligo interrupted, with an incredulous titter. "Then his Royal owner decides on any punishment. Good Lord, what could Mummy want with him?"

"Not Mummy… I mean not the Queen, your highness."

"Not my sister?" Caligo's crimson gaze widened in amusement as the Head Foreman nodded. "So much for that surd rights, anti-ownership nonsense she used to spout. She's obviously grown up and learned a bit of sense since I last saw her. Good for her."

"But, my Prince," Perval said. "He's dangerous, a murderer—"

"Then he'll fit in well at the palace. The courtiers and their servants are venomous snakes, the lot of them."

"But, your highness—"

"Enough!" The murderous red of Caligo's eyes seemed to bloody further, as his anger rose and congealed. "You were a faithful chamber boy during my years at the military academy and have served me again by inviting me here. You are right, these are excellent workers. For that, I am thankful. But do not let my gratitude confuse you. I will not argue with someone as insignificant as a failed guard, however helpful he may have been to me. Is that clear?"

As all eyes took in Perval's humiliation, he muttered out a pinched, "Yes, my Prince." Frank psychically willed him to look his way. His wish granted, Perval turned his gaze to the floor in his embarrassment.

Drool or no drool, Frank smirked the smuggest smirk he could manage.

Perval's mouth puckered shut like a constipated arsehole and Frank knew he had won whatever battle they'd been fighting. He'd be free of him and leaving for the palace, no less. He was curious why he had been chosen, of course, but stranger things had happened recently and he was not about to argue against what sounded like a definite step up. If he had anything to bet with, he'd wager there wasn't a drop of caenosa milk to be found in the entire palace. And maybe he could help Seph feed...

"Cragor, my best worker, and these final few," the Head Foreman said, ticking off the final names. "That's the lot of them. May they serve you well, your highness."

"Cra... Cra..." was all Frank managed as the guards herded the condemned men away. Perval shot him a last spiteful smirk as he followed.

Cragor hesitated in the doorway with a sad expression in his eyes, ignoring the guard half his size trying to shove him forward. "Take care of Tulip for me. And tell Seph..."

Frank never heard what he would say to Seph. A zap of the guard's baton was not enough to fell the might of Cragor, but it stole his words, prodded him on and away. By the time Frank regained his strength, the men and the train that carried them were long gone.

The next few hours passed in a blur as Frank

withdrew into himself, his tasered mind drifting between confusion, sadness, and a paralysing panic. He couldn't remember being taken to the train, could barely focus on the colours of the city whipping by.

But when he saw the palace, he couldn't help but gasp.

The grand castle, and its many spires and parapets, was built entirely from gemstones, larger and more brilliant than any he had heard tale of above. Most of the walls were made of a pale sparkling citrine and peridot. The gatehouses were constructed of giant blocks of sapphire with portcullises of silver. Amethyst turrets jutted from tower after tower. One huge rose diamond sat atop the highest pinnacle.

As the guards handed him over to the palace soldiers, he feared the place more than he ever had the Barn. He could see why Cragor hated royals.

How could anyone live in such callous grandeur when others starved as they worked? And what could such a person want with him?

With no choice but to follow as ordered, he allowed himself to be led inside. Most of the troop ignored him, as though he were nothing more than a package being delivered. Except one. The guard in front of him turned for a split second as another knocked on the palace door. He was older, perhaps the oldest soldier there, not elderly but reaching late middle age, the bags beneath his green eyes sagging. He stared directly at Frank for a moment, then turned away like nothing had happened. The door opened, and the soldiers handed him over to a butler, liveried in gold cloth and ruby buttons.

"You are now the servant of the Princess, beloved daughter of our Majesty, Queen Gaeatrix. When you enter her chamber, remain silent, and do not raise your eyes from the ground until you are

THOSE OF THE LIGHT

spoken to. Is that understood?"

He nodded. He followed the butler up a grand moonstone staircase, trying to rub dried milk from his overalls.

As they stepped through a wide archway, Frank bowed his head and looked at the floor.

"Your purchase, your highness," the butler announced. The Princess must have dismissed him with a gesture. The butler retreated with a bow, the doors closing behind him.

Silence reigned for a moment as Frank felt the Princess assess him, wandering around him, eyeing his body.

"Cute butt," the Princess said.

He looked up to find purple eyes.

"Hi," Seph said.

NICOLA CURRIE

7

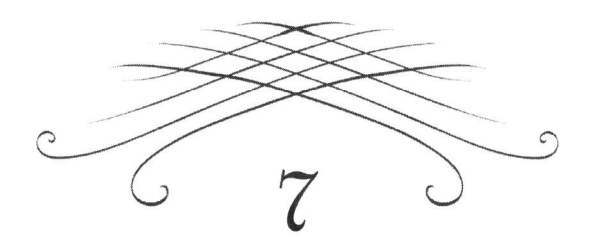

"You're the princess?"

To be fair, she looked the part. Her choppy bob was slicked back and jewelled with crystal flowers. Instead of overalls, she wore a black silk wrap dress that trailed to the floor, a slit revealing one leg. Her diamond mouths studs were the only element of her ensemble he recognised, which, now he thought about it, should have made him realise from the beginning that Seph was not an ordinary woman, to be sparkle adorned in a world such as this.

Her room was huge. A massive four-poster bed dressed with rich velvets and satins covered around a tenth of the shortest wall. Opposite, row after row of open closets housed hundreds of fine gowns, their enamel frames engraved with intricate golden roses and silver lilies. At the room's centre, wide steps led to a vast balcony, the view beneath it revealing all the lights and colours of the city, its grids and curves and tracks mapped as far as the eye could see.

No wonder Seph seemed to know everything about everything. There it was, all laid at her feet.

"That's Princess Persephone to you, kid." She tried to say it with her usual tone of light-hearted mockery, but here, like this, she somehow couldn't pull it off.

It wasn't the gorgeous palace, the fine clothes, the furnishings, and gemstones that made Seph seem different here.

Frank had never seen her look this vulnerable.

She moved differently too, he noticed, as she walked over to a side table and poured herself a glass of almost black liquid, swallowing it quickly, as though looking for courage at the bottom. She was stiffer, meeker than the scrappy Seph he knew, holding herself in, playing a role that didn't suit her.

She didn't belong here anymore than he did.

"This must be a bit of surprise," Seph said, pouring herself another glass. "How rude of me. Stoneberry wine?"

Frank needed a little courage too, and a few minutes more to figure out the kindest way to break her heart. He nodded and took the drink gladly. It was better than any wine he had ever tasted, of sweet blackcurrant contrasted with stone and earth. It was too celebratory for the news he had to share, but he drained it to the last drop, finding no answers.

"I guess it's obvious now that my situation is complicated," she began, fidgeting her fingers nervously against her glass in a way that was so unSeph-like. "Cragor said enough the other night to tell you why I didn't say anything before. I've always worried he wouldn't understand. I'm not like them, you see. My mother and brother. Never have been. I never understood how it could be right for us to have everything while people like Cragor... Well, you've seen for yourself. I've spent my life hating how my family prefer to rule in the dark when we could all be free together in the light."

He had thought Seph had a streak of rebelliousness from the moment he saw her studs and fondness for black when he awoke in the hospital; a moment that felt long ago now. But he could never have imagined how deep that feeling went, how it could define her whole life, splitting it into two opposite halves. Seph of the streets and secrets. Persephone of the gemstone palace.

"I hope you can forgive me," she said, sad-eyed,

biting her lip in a way so childlike, he forgave her without even knowing why he needed to. "I swore I would never buy out anyone's debt. A part of me wanted to, all the years I've known Cragor. I could give him almost anything he could desire. But then, legally, I'd own him. I don't think he could live with that. I know I could never live with myself."

"But last night," Seph continued, "I realised who Perval was. The name rang in my head like an alarm all the way home. I knew I'd heard it somewhere before. Then it clicked. When I snuck into my brother's old tower and found his photos from school, that confirmed it. Perval was my brother's bitch, years ago. Then, though I always say no, Mother asked me if I wanted to join her for lunch the next day. Caligo was visiting the city, she said, and, of course, together they think they have a better chance of convincing me to see things the way they do, to agree to…well, that's beside the point. I knew something was up. My brother rarely comes to the city and not without a reason. When I asked about his itinerary and your particular barn was mentioned, I had a hunch things would soon go very wrong for you. From the state of you, I guess I was right."

"You were and I'm grateful, but Seph—"

She was excited now, pacing, freed from her secret to be the dynamic Seph he knew.

"I have to tell Cragor soon if we're going to move fast, but I need a few more days to set things in motion, then I can—"

"Set what in motion? Cragor's—"

"Everyone will want to meet you before they'll accept the plan—"

"Seph!"

Egalitarian as she was in her heart, he knew from the shocked look on her face she was not used to being yelled at.

"What?" she said, still brimming with her cryptic excitement. "Don't you see? We never had a way before, but you, you're the key, Dreamer. Cragor will be happy it's finally happening. He'll understand that I've always been Seph, never Persephone and soon, I can be his Seph forever."

"But that's the problem," Frank murmured, the guilt his now, knowing her heart was about to crumble before him. "He's gone. Cragor's gone."

They sat on the steps in silence for some time after he had finished explaining what had happened at the Barn that day, drinking the last of the stoneberry wine. Seph's blank-eyed quiet was worse than the fury and tears he had imagined.

"Cragor's stronger than any man I've met above or below," Frank said eventually, unable to bear the silence any longer. "He can survive anything, for a little while anyway. We'll come up with a plan."

"A plan," Seph said wistfully. "I had a plan. The

best plan we have ever had. I thought this one had a good chance. That it would happen. I suppose it still can, for the others. But not for me, not without Cragor."

Seph stood and drifted over to her bed, a ghost of herself. She pressed a small button and a distant bell sounded somewhere.

"I'm tired," she said, getting into bed, fully clothed. "So tired." A servant appeared in the doorway. "Please show my…my… Please take him to his room. And bring me more wine."

Frank didn't want to leave her, as his family had not wanted to leave him when Nora was first lost to him. But he also knew she needed time to cry, to panic, to come back to herself.

He followed the footman through the palace, hating himself a little more with every step. He would end this strange day in more opulence and grandeur than he could ever have imagined, while

Cragor descended to a fate darker than anyone deserved, and him least of all.

Sure enough, even the servants' chambers were like decent hotel rooms. But as he sank onto his new double bed, exhausted, he knew he'd exchange it for his crappy hammock in a second, if it meant this could all be a bad dream.

Frank couldn't sleep, guilt running through him like too much caffeine. This would have never happened to Cragor if not for him.

No. If not for Perval.

Guilt was replaced with a red-hot anger. Thoughts of Cragor's hell didn't leave his mind for a moment and when Frank fell asleep, he raged through nightmare landscapes of fire, searching for his friend, burning too.

NICOLA CURRIE

8

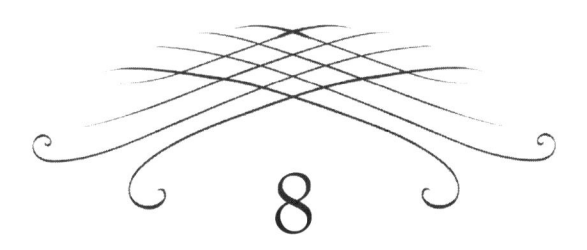

Frank rested fitfully and was surprised to find someone had visited his room overnight without disturbing him. Clean clothes had been hung in the wardrobe opposite his bed and Tulip slept in her cage on a table. Seph must have sent a servant to bring her to him, knowing Cragor wouldn't want her to be left all alone.

When he'd showered and dressed in jeans and a shirt, he stepped out into the hallway. Other servants, some liveried, some not, passed by, heading towards the sound of clattering plates and conversation at the end of the corridor. Frank was pretty sure this was 'below stairs' as they said in the period dramas Nora used to like, in the basements of the palace. He wanted to go to Seph but had to play his part, had to remember hers. He could only wait until he was summoned. He followed the others, glad to find a breakfast of eggs, bacon, and coffee waiting. He took the opportunity to eat his fill, knowing Cragor would have done the same.

As he lay down his knife and fork, someone stopped at his table. He looked up. He recognised the palace soldier who had stared at him the evening before. His green eyes glinted in amusement as they noticed Frank's bloated belly.

"It seems Sir's breakfast is satisfactory," he said. "But I am afraid I must disturb you from it. The Princess has instructed me to accompany you to your new work placement, in the royal botanical garden. Follow me, Sir."

Sir? It seemed circumstances had changed more than he had realised. He outranked a soldier? As he followed him through the palace, other servants reacted to Frank too. Footmen and scullery maids bowed and curtsied. Corridor guards hopped to one side when they approached, as precisely as automatic doors. The snotty butler from the night before shook his hand like an equal, inviting him for whisky and cigars in his apartment at the day's end.

Who am I now? Not that it mattered. Frank trusted Seph and would play whatever part she needed him to play.

They stepped out into the rear courtyard. As they climbed a rocky incline that led up from the farthest side, heading towards the edge of the great cavern, the soldier dropped back and walked next to him.

"Is it true?" A boyish look of wonder transformed the soldier's wrinkled face. "Did you really survive the drop while awake?"

"Well, I wasn't awake all of the time, but I suppose so," Frank answered, not understanding why that mattered. It had interested Seph too. "Why is that such a big deal?"

The man lost the last of his military decorum and practically skipped up the rest of the slope until they approached a plateau. Beyond it, a narrow tunnel, only wide enough for foot traffic, led away into the rock.

"Because it means Seph's right," the man said, catching his breath as they reached the top of the incline and stepped up onto the flat shelf above. "You could be it. You could be the answer we've been waiting for."

"Answer to what?" Frank asked. One thing he had learned since descending—since he'd met powerful Cragor, shrewd Seph, cruel Perval, even diva Tulip—was that he, Frank, was quite unspecial. The only quality he had in super abundance was love for Nora. He hoped Nora knew that, wherever she was, and still wanted him, but it baffled him why anyone else would.

"Seph can explain it better than I can, it's her idea." The man beamed. "But it could work, with enough luck and courage. Even if it's risky, how much longer are we going to wait? I'm getting old and I've been dreaming of it all my three hundred and seventy-two years. I have to try while I still can. If I die in the process, so be it."

"I wish I knew what was going on," Frank huffed, frustrated with the way people here spoke in riddles. This wasn't a game, and every second wasted was an insult to Cragor's and Tilourik's suffering.

"The Princess insisted we all gather, so she could explain her plan to everyone at once. A little further, Sir."

"Why do you keep calling me, Sir? And who are

you, while we're at it?" Frank had never sounded so much like an uppity Sir in his life.

"Apologies, Sir, I'm Rockford, Sir, one of the Princess's personal guards. I have been since the day she was born. Not that she's let any of us do much guarding for some time. I'm obliged to address all the Chiefs of the Royal Estate as Sir. You may recall me referring to the butler as Sir, as Chief of the Palace. In your role, as Chief of the Gardens, I must show you the same courtesy."

"I'm Chief of the what now?"

Rockford pointed to the tunnel and walked towards it, urging him to follow. It was low, just tall enough for him to enter without stooping. It twisted around a corner so he couldn't see where it led, despite the lights embedded directly into the rock above their heads. He wondered how far the tunnel could go on for if it relied on so many little bulbs.

But when they turned the bend, he was dazzled.

The tunnel already widened out a little and was lit on both sides by bushes covered by the strangest, most stunning flower.

They were luminous, emitting light where there was none. Their petals were edged with silver but otherwise similar in shape and colouring to the snowdrops Frank used to get in his garden every spring. A heavenly glow emanated out of them, illuminating the way ahead, to a gate guarded by two soldiers in the distance.

Such a rare bloom was the first thing he had seen below that was truly, purely, beautiful.

"Umbra Iubar," Rockford said. "Also known as Shadow's Radiance. Careful, don't…"

Frank yanked his fingers back from the silken petals just in time, as the flower's bell opened and sharp fangs snapped out.

"…touch."

Of course it has teeth. Frank watched a moth,

drawn to the light, land on a petal only to be swallowed whole. Every deal had its drawbacks down here, it would seem, kind of like how an extra four hundred years of unexpected life was hardly working out to be a bed of roses. Unless those roses were covered in manure.

"This the national flower, is it?"

"Why, yes," Rockford said. "But how did you know?"

"Just a hunch."

Rockford needed to rush ahead but Frank took his time passing through the rest of the tunnel, making sure he stayed in the centre of the path. The flowers snapped out at him anyway and he regretted his big breakfast and the inches of bloat it had given him. He was relieved when he reached the end and saw that the space widened out into a cavern beyond.

Words wrought into the ironwork at the top of

the gate said: *The Glade.*

Like the others in the palace, the soldiers stood aside and saluted as he passed. He tapped his bracelet on the entry panel, certain he would be denied and the soldiers would drag him off, realising there had been some mistake. Yet the gate swung open, and he stepped out onto a floor of lush green that he assumed must be artificial.

But here, while the killer flowers lit the borders of the space, it was the rays that shone from above that illuminated, that nourished.

Sunlight.

The space was barely bigger than a football pitch on the ground, but vertically, it could have held a cathedral. Light streamed from a crack in the centre of the ceiling, its spotlight falling on the only grass Frank had seen grow down here, on flowers he recognised from his life above. Seph stood beneath the golden glow, bathing in it.

"It's not quite real," Seph said. "It's not direct sunlight, anyway. It's refracted a thousand times as it is funnelled from far above through a hundred different channels. meeting and concentrating on this very spot. Still, it's my favourite place in the whole kingdom."

She closed her arms and savoured it, like she was in the middle of a warm hug.

As Frank approached, she bent and picked one of the pink flowers that bloomed there. A tulip.

"I brought Cragor one of these once. They're his favourite flower, though he'd only seen them in pictures before that. He wanted to see how it grew. But I can't bring anyone I please into the palace grounds, especially not a barn worker, and definitely not one that stands out as much as he does. But it didn't matter, I told him. He'd see the real thing for himself, sprouting from the ground. When we were free. When we were up there."

So that was what Seph wanted, all along. It made sense. Who got nearer to the surface, nearer to those freshly descended from above, than a greeter? Who had better travel clearance than the Princess, to explore whatever options could be found for escape?

And yet, in her one hundred and twenty-six years, she had not managed it. That did not fill him with hope. Then he recalled what he had seen on the back of her neck and, if he was correct, what it might mean. How much bigger it could all be.

"What does your tattoo say?"

Seph smiled in happy surprise. "Impressive. You're obviously smarter than you look."

She turned and flipped up her hair.

Her tattoo was a half-circle with angled lines that rayed out above it and to the sides, like a sun rising over a horizon. Beneath it, three letters: L S R.

He was right. Seph wasn't just his streetwise

friend, wasn't just a princess.

She was a Light Seeker.

And from the fight in her eyes when she dropped her hair and turned back, Frank could see the true rebellion was about to begin.

9

"The others are waiting," Seph said. "They want to understand the part you're going to play. As I'm sure you do too. This way."

She walked towards a far corner of the glade, where there was nothing but a brick well.

"In here."

"In where?"

A second later, Seph was gone. She had swung her legs over the side and dropped into it. He heard a light splash as she landed in the water.

"Seph!" Frank ran to the hole and looked over. Below, he only saw black.

"It's okay," her voiced echoed from the darkness. "Reach under the ledge. Feel for the top of the rope hidden there. Then jump in and let your hands slide down it. It's not far, I promise."

In usual circumstances, he would have no intention of flinging himself into an unlit shaft of unknown depth, but after his close shave at the Barn and the threat of flesh-eating flowers, this wasn't the biggest challenge he had faced in the last twenty-four hours. And from the sound of things, he might find answers at the bottom. He grabbed the rope, jumping into the well before he had a chance to feel afraid.

Seph was right; it wasn't far, three metres or so. The water came up to his knees, which would have been fine if he hadn't slipped when his feet met the wet stones below. His head went under with the rest of his body, shocked by the cold. When he spluttered to the surface, he saw Seph standing to the side of the pool, lantern in hand, dry as a bone from her boots up. The space behind her glowed with a light that Frank hoped suggested a warm room beyond.

"You need to work on your landing, kid." She pulled him back to his feet, then stepped through a doorway. He followed quickly, before the light of the lantern left with her. "You can dry off here. Join us when you're ready."

They had entered a small room with a large fireplace hewn into the rock. Above it, the dawning sun symbol of the Light Seekers had been engraved into the stone. Several pairs of wet shoes and trousers on a rail dried in front of crackling flames. An odd assortment of spare clothes—jeans, t-shirts, jumpers, socks—were jumbled in an open trunk to one side. He stripped to his underwear and warmed himself for a few minutes. Stone steps led downwards and round to the right. He could hear voices greeting, questioning. When he had hung his clothes up to dry and helped himself to new ones, Frank descended the stairs, the voices falling silent as he turned the corner.

"Is that him?" a saggy-jowled, curly grey-haired woman said. "He doesn't look like any kind of hero to me."

Rude.

Though, to be fair, Frank was wearing a canary-yellow jumper and checked flares, which, despite his best rummage through the trunk, was the most sensible clothing available. Light Seekers clearly had a sense of humour.

Besides, it was not like the rest of them could talk. He'd never seen such a bizarre mix of people. There were two dozen or so. Most sat in rows of chairs, like it was a meeting of Weirdos

Anonymous. Some looked tough and grey-toned, like Cragor; others had eyes of deep black and red. At a rectangular stone table on a platform at the front, an odd couple sat with Seph, Rockford, and Mrs Rude Jowl Face. They were dressed in black Victorian garb, their red surd monitoring bracelets excepted, apparently having had no interest in keeping up with fashion in the many years since they had descended from the surface.

The room was strange too. Even in candlelight, he could make out caveman-like paintings on the walls, the ceiling, the floor. Each depicted a story of the sun: a sun above blooming fields; a sun above dancing children; a sun twinned with its lover moon. Each was a prayer, a wish. It was sad to see them drawn so faintly now, crumbled away over time. Prayers that had never come true.

"Hero might be pushing it," Seph admitted with a smile. "Frank, please join us. Take a seat next to

Wendamel. Don't worry, she's only mean to people who interest her."

He walked to the table and sat next to his new friend, smiling. Wendamel scowled at him, jowls shaking with something like distrust or annoyance. Or both.

Her eyes narrowed further.

Probably both.

"It is a mere thirty months," Seph began, "until we reach the date we set twenty years ago; a deadline by which we pledged—to each other, to you all—to find a way to the surface, before this resurrected group marks its two hundred and fiftieth anniversary under the second rebellion. While we…"

"That's how long it's been since I discovered this temple," Rockford whispered, leaning across the table. "Fell down the well after too many welcoming ciders my first night after joining the palace barracks. When I found the book, and the truth of what really happened during the surface occupation war, I restarted the new rebellion from that day to this. Thought I was a dead man when the Princess learned about it, but you know our Seph. A fighter and an angel, all in one. Quickly became the best leader we could hope for."

"…after so many disappointments, we have struggled to believe we would ever find a way. I believe with Frank's help, we have."

The Victorian gentleman held a monocle between one round black cheek and brow. "The man's too puny and small of forehead to possess the strength or intellect of an engineer, so one can only assume that escape plan m21 isn't the winning solution, and he hasn't invented a silent boring machine that would allow us to drill our way up to the surface undetected. I must say, I'm glad. That was my least favourite. All that disturbed earth would get frightfully messy."

"Perhaps, dear Rupert, he is an inventor, and has invented a submersible small enough but strong enough to transport us through the depths of the underground sea, into the currents that would carry us out via a fissure to the higher waters, where the oceans below become the oceans above."

"Plan s14 was always your preference, Lillibet, but he has not the air of a great inventor about him. Tell me, good sir, what is your occupation?"

Frank tried not to frown. It might make his small forehead shrink even further.

"Um… I managed a supermarket," he said. The silence that followed was tinged with a sense of anti-climax.

Again, rude. His aisles had been the most well-organised in the East of England.

"But he is so much more than that," Seph said. "He's a dreamer."

There was a collective gasp, like she had cast some spell with the mere mention of a magical word.

Rupert adjusted his monocle and leaned towards him. "But he doesn't appear to be deranged or deformed."

"Take off your clothes and prove it."

"He's not taking off his clothes, Wendamel. You can't tell every new member to take off their clothes, we've talked about this."

"He could be a spy. There could be a recorder in his pants."

"There's nothing in his pants—"

"Hey!" Frank said. "Will you both stop discussing my pants and what is or isn't inside them? I don't have to put up with any of this, you know. I could leave right now."

"You could," Seph said, rolling her eyes at both him and Wendamel, who was now tugging at his trousers. "But without the travel clearance and resources I'm going to give you, how will you find your wife?"

He froze, no longer caring about Wendamel's wandering hands, or Rupert's insulting pseudoscientific judgements.

"Ready to shut up and listen? All of you?" Seph sounded like an exhausted schoolteacher. "I don't want to hear a word until I've explained."

An incoherent grumble rumbled around the room, but it murmured into silence.

"I've always felt like the best plan was the easiest plan. As well as platforms that carry surds down when their time above is over, we know there are platforms that also go up, delivering goods to the surface. They're crawling with government agents and guards, sure, but what about the ones no longer in service? We've discussed this plan before—"

"Plan p77," Rupert interrupted, blushing when

he saw he had earned himself a look of purple daggers.

"—which we dismissed," Seph continued, "because of a small but important detail. One of us would need to stay awake, to make sure we got there safely and to rouse us when we reached the surface. But the only way we could make it through such a journey without going mad is if we were heavily sedated. We talked about taking sedatives at different times, so we only had to be awake a few hours each, in shifts. With no accurate idea of how long it could take and a strong chance the velocity would knock us all out, regardless, that would be too risky. We knew no one could survive for the duration. And then Frank did."

This announcement elicited no gasp, the breath of each Light Seeker caught in their chests. Instead, everyone's gaze turned to Frank, their bodies otherwise frozen in excitement. Even Wendamel stopped stroking his thigh, which, to his surprise, he found disappointing. It had been a very long time.

"It's impossible," Rupert said, wide-eyed beneath his monocle. "And one so clearly feeble of brain, too. How on earth did you manage it, boy?"

"Um, dunno…" he said, sounding feeble of brain. He didn't do anything but what he always did: think of Nora.

Perhaps that was the answer. She had been the one that spurred him on, in this life and the one they shared before.

Maybe this was the chance he had been waiting for. A chance to find his Nora and live their life over. Above.

"What about Nora? If this is your price, I'll do it, but then Nora comes too."

Seph's face softened. "Of course she does. And I didn't mean it to sound like that. A price. I'd help you find Nora whether you said yes or no, I hope

THOSE OF THE LIGHT

you know that. But when you do find her, this is the only way any of us can be free."

"It won't work," a black-eyed guy with black spiky hair said from the second row. "Do you think they'll let us get away with it? That no one will come after us?"

"We've thought of that," Seph said, turning to Wendamel, who nodded, jowls wobbling in agreement. "Wend's been promoted to Senior Curator at the Bioancestral Archive. If we time it right, she can delete us from every record there is, and we'll be gone before anyone notices. Untraceable. It will take some precision. Rockford is analysing guard surveillance patterns, catching up with his old guard chums, trying to establish routes to our potential exit points that will have the fewest checkpoints and guard stations. Lillibet has infiltrated state government offices and is slowly securing blueprints, manuals and consignment plans so we can find out which platform tunnels are no longer in use and how to operate them."

"They think I'm just a stupid temp," Lillibet tittered. "Little do they know that every time I visit the lavatory, I am sewing more photocopies into my petticoats. It is most amusing."

"There are lots of other pieces that need to fall into place too," Seph admitted. "But we can do it. I know we can. But we have to move fast. We don't have thirty months anymore. We have a week. Some of our friends were taken to the Pit. One of them knew about our plans and there is information in the Pit that could help us, too. He'll know what to look for. He won't last long there, so it's now or never."

Frank wondered if that was true or if Seph would risk everything, everyone, for Cragor. He suspected it might be half of one and some of the other. She glanced at him like they were sharing a secret. He understood. He'd do it for Nora.

"So, make your preparations and get ready to move at a moment's notice. We'll keep you updated on our final plan through the usual channels. With luck on our side, this could be the last meeting the LSR ever have. I wish you sunlight."

The group parted with shared farewells of *I wish you sunlight*. Further doorways at the far back of the room led to further passageways and, Frank presumed, further hidden entrances beyond.

Wendamel stood and grabbed his face, still scowling at him. He was sure she was going to slap him.

"I wish you..." she said. She paused and leaned in menacingly. Before he could catch his breath, she planted a smacker of a kiss on his lips. "...sunlight," she said when she was finished, the cheeky lopsided smile she gave him before she walked away suggesting she had wished for something else altogether.

When he had recovered, Frank thought about what an interesting day it had been. He'd become a royal gardener, an integral part of a centuries' old rebellion and the crush of a horny four-hundred-year-old woman, all in the space of a few hours.

Life is full of surprises.

When only Frank, Rockford, and Seph remained, Seph grabbed the monitor on his wrist, scanning it with hers.

"Like I said, I hope you know I'd help you, no matter what. As royal gardener, you have much better clearance now. You can travel into the city. If Nora was bought out, she'll most likely be in one of the bar or pleasure districts, so you should start there. Rockford's agreed to come with you, with twenty of his best men. You'll cover the clubs and bars much quicker that way. I've told Mother I commissioned a new fountain, in honour of my…well, it means you need men to help you collect materials. I've topped up your credits, too. Pay whatever tips you must to get answers. And have a beer while you're at it. After the time you've had recently, you deserve one."

He followed Seph and Rockford towards the steps that led to the fire above and the well beyond. He paused at the edge of the temple and looked back at the ancient stone, the carved hopes, the silence of the room echoing with ghosts. He wondered how many had been there before him, how many had yearned for the life he had been so lucky to have.

He'd have it again. They all would. Even if he had to gamble with his last breath.

NICOLA CURRIE

10

"So, the government lied?" Frank whispered. Rockford had said he couldn't be sure who to trust, even amongst his most loyal men. It wasn't wise to speak ill of the Queen. "That's hardly mind blowing. That's what they do, the world over."

Once he had changed into a fresh set of clothes, he had followed Rockford onto a train headed into the heart of the city, the promised men in tow. What a difference it was. When he entered the carriage, the other passengers no longer spurned and shunned him. They moved to make room as soon as they saw he led a troop of palace soldiers and gave up their seats with respectful nods. Seph had made him somebody, though Frank didn't particularly like their deference, either. He didn't want to be somebody in this world. He wanted to be Frank and Nora in the world he knew.

As the train passed the skyscrapers of the business district, each floor of its towers studded with white lights, Rockford told him about the ancient book he had found, dust-covered on the temple's stone table. *Herein lies the buried truth* was etched on its cover.

There had been a surface occupation war, that much was true, Rockford had explained. It wasn't because it was too unsafe to stay above though. The dangers had long since passed. An equilibrium had been achieved as people moved freely between above and below, attracted to new opportunities underground but not shut away from the light. They could return to the surface as they pleased.

"Of course they lied," Rockford replied. "When the rich and powerful realised how much control they had over people underground, they became greedy, as the rich and powerful are wont to do. Life below was more dangerous, so there had to be more controls. Travel restrictions. Strict monitoring. Complicated license requirements for marriages and the right to have children. They knew if they forced everyone to live below their power would be absolute. So, they spread their propaganda, decried the selfishness of those that wished to live above and started their war. They won easily: the pact was another lie. The Light Seekers who weren't executed were enslaved instead, as much above as their descendants now are below. Over time, they twisted and manipulated stories so the society that regrew above didn't know their bodies were being aged, diseased, sped towards endless servitude in a hidden world they no longer knew existed."

Frank had never known his parents. There were no names except Mother Superior's signature at the bottom of his birth certificate, and his place of birth was noted to be an East London orphanage. Yet he burned with fury for them. He always hoped they had a good life, a peaceful death, but now he knew. Whoever they were, they suffered. In all probability, they continued to suffer. And that was the fate of everyone he had ever known.

The train was slowing now. He could see swarms of people below as it passed over a bridge above their heads. The busy street shone in shades of electric blue and neon pink, the signs above bars, casinos, and restaurants flashing, creating an atmosphere part alien, part 1980s. The people were similarly strange and colourful, wearing clothes from every century Frank knew from his history above as well as millennia from some future time surds like him had never known; outfits that varied between androgynous, hyperfeminine, hypermasculine, or some juxtaposed combination, all aswirl with shapes more suitable for architecture than fashion. Their hairstyles were creative, too, tangled and straightened into a variety of silky cascades and elaborate bouffants. There were eyes of brown, red, black, and white.

None like Seph's though, he realised, as they stepped off the platform and exited a small station onto the bustling street. He was proud that someone special in so many ways needed him so much. But another needed him more and as he surveyed the road that stretched endlessly into the distance, he wondered if he had a chance of finding her.

"Where do we begin?" Frank asked. "There are hundreds of venues, thousands."

"Pleasure Mile's got a lot going on, I'll give you

that," Rockford said. "But it's where almost all surd women who get bought out of factory jobs end up. It's our best bet. My men and I can work through most of it, at least asking if anyone's heard of her. Half of us will search the left side and the other half, the right. You take the central square. That should keep you busy for a few hours. We'll find you there. Come on, boys."

Rockford and his men split off to opposite sides and disappeared into the crowd. Frank walked towards the square, jostled as endless streams of people laughed and rushed and barged past him. He could tell the difference between them already. The ones with the most expressive hairstyles or expensive suits, the groups of business professionals and clichés of entitled kids, and the ones that could enter fine restaurants with 'no surds' on the window all wore metallic bracelets. The street food vendors and waste disposal workers, the badged bar tenders and waitresses, and the others that looked as lost and desperate as he felt, had wrists wrapped with red.

"Birds of Paradise!" a man said, handing him a card. "Home to the most beautiful naked surd women in Pleasure Mile. That card will get you a free cocktail with any lap dance."

"Yeah, thanks," Frank said dismissively, slipping it into his pocket. As he approached the square, everybody seemed to want to give him something, or to encourage him inside each establishment he passed. Within minutes, he was promised a foursome with blonde triplets (buy two get one free), a discounted naked hugging session buried in what were supposedly the Mile's most famous huge bosoms, and as much penis as he could want (Frank's answer: none). Street vendors offered him gigantic southern fried spider's legs, curried lizard, and caenosa ice cream (*Nope!*). Everything was bizarre, eye-opening, and terrifying.

The bars and strip clubs were no different. He had seen some things in his time, but after searching the first few venues and seeing what he saw there, he was a changed man.

How do they get their legs to bend that way?

After exploring one side of the square, he was starting to despair and paused for a moment at a bench. In the last place, a gentleman's club where the waitresses wore nothing but masquerade masks, the barman gave him hope when he told him they had a girl called Nora. But when she sauntered over, he could tell it wasn't his wife before she took off her mask. He was disappointed and relieved at the same time.

He glanced around at the rest of the square, planning his next steps. One club stood out among the many. Sequined lights in the shape of a giant toucan and the words 'Birds of Paradise' shone above the wide entrance. It was bold and garish, dominating amongst all the colour and noise. Nonetheless, it didn't hold his attention for long. He was far more interested in the person he spotted entering its doors.

Perval.

So this is what he gets up to when he comes to the city.

Frank crossed the square and shadowed him inside. They entered a large lobby lined by at least three dozen oversized portraits of beautiful women, stretching to the floor and serving as painted doorways. They were tastefully nude but provocative, catering to a range of kinks and fetishes, from demure babydolled beauties to hand-tied submissives. As he passed through, a 50s-styled high-heeled stunner, dressed in a parrot printed pencil skirt and bralette, escorted a man to one of the doors. When she ushered him in, Frank caught a glimpse of a whip-equipped dominatrix inside.

"Looking for a good time, hunny?" The woman said with a generous, red-lipped smile, noticing Frank as she closed the door. "You'd better sign up fast. Our ladies are almost booked up for the night."

"Could you tell me if there is a woman called Nora here?"

"Sorry, sweetie, Nora isn't available. She's exclusively reserved. If any of the other ladies take your fancy, let me know."

"Wait, where…" But the hostess had already moved on.

His pulse was racing, and he almost tripped as he rushed into the heart of the club. It wasn't what he expected. Scantily clad women shimmered on platforms, sure, but the place had an elegance to it. More like a ballroom than a club, smartly dressed circular tables wrapped around a small dance floor, facing a stage at the front with a curtain of bright

THOSE OF THE LIGHT

feathers. To the left of the room was a long black bar that had a real toucan on a perch in the back.

Perval sat on a stool at the end nearest the stage, talking to a man behind the bar. He wasn't uniformed in bird print like the other bar staff and hostesses. This was a man in charge. Frank sat at a table nearby, hidden by a leafy green plant, and watched as Perval held out his bracelet. The bartender tapped his against it and nodded, like some deal was made, some credits exchanged.

Frank's mind leapt at an explanation that left him tingling with both rage and hope. Perval had recognised his name that first day at the Barn. Nora was reserved for someone. Exclusive. Perval hated him with a furious jealousy, as though he coveted something that belonged to Frank.

As music started, Perval spun in his seat and faced the stage as the curtain parted, his face as eager as a humping dog. Frank followed his gaze and knew he was right.

There she was.

His Nora.

She stood in front of a microphone in a sparkly red dress. He was so transfixed by how young she looked, how beautiful, with her chestnut hair waved in that way he had always liked. It took him a moment to recognise the song. When Nora started to sing Billie Holiday, he was so in love he didn't think he was capable of holding it, his heart a balloon about to burst.

The room, the city, the whole dark deep world disappeared as she sang. It was her and him once more, seventy years melting away, like he was a kid again, standing in the dance hall where he saw her for the first time, willing her to look at him. She hadn't looked at him then either, and now, as Perval clapped and cheered inelegantly from the side, she stared at the floor, occasionally closing her eyes, perhaps thinking of the same dance hall Frank did.

When she finished the song, Nora accepted the rapturous applause with a gentle curtsy, then exited the stage without looking at anyone. She was so far away from the bright, outgoing Nora he knew, it worried him. What had she been through in the two years she'd spent here alone?

Perval hopped from his stool and walked past the end of the bar to a curtained door to the front left of the stage. Frank followed, stopping at the bar, hiding behind a menu, listening. Two suited men, almost as big as Cragor, guarded the way. One held up a hand as Perval approached.

"Nora said she'll be ready in a bit. You'll have to wait here until she calls for you."

"Calls for me?" Perval said, sneering. "Maybe you should remind Nora I'm the only reason she hasn't been fucked by every one of the club's regulars. Most of the girls get through them in a month. She needs to remember how lucky she was to have a good guy like me as her first customer. Someone willing to protect her, to be patient. Very patient. Tell her I mean it. She'll have to show me more respect when she's my wife."

The two men burst into loud, mocking laughter, one of them clutching his side.

"Nora? Marry you?" the other one said. "You can't get pussy in a whorehouse when you're paying for it and you think she's going to marry you? That's hilarious."

"We're just waiting," Perval said, through gritted teeth. "Nora's mine."

"Nora's still hung up on her husband. Everyone knows that. I can't see the girl without hearing Frank this and Frank that. That's a loyal wife, if there ever was one. When I got here six years after my wife, she'd already remarried and didn't recognise me until I explained. It worked out alright in the end when…"

As the bouncers kept Perval distracted with further insults and humiliations, Frank knew he had to get to Nora first. He walked along the bar, to the centre, where the man he had identified as the one in charge was feeding his toucan bites of banana.

"How much to see Nora?" Frank said to him, leaning over the bar.

"Sorry, buddy," the man said, without taking his eyes away from his bird. "She's not available. She's a one guy kind of gal."

"I know. I'm Frank."

The man scoffed. "Sure you are, buddy. You're the fifth one this week." He closed the bird back in his cage and turned around. He placed both hands on the bar and leaned forward, his face inches away from Frank's. "It's common knowledge that Frank was the name of Nora's husband on the surface and that she's holding on to her naïve little hope that she'll find him, so everything will be hunky-dory, the same as it was up there. She's business to me, sure, but I happen to like the girl and I'm sick of seeing her heartbreak every time it turns out it ain't him because some idiot's lied to get close to her. So get lost."

"But I really am Frank! Look, I'll make a deal with you. I'll pay you for one minute with her so she can confirm who I am. You keep the money either way."

The man sighed, straightened, and poured himself a whisky. "Listen, I don't know what your deal is, but I have a customer who pays a generous holding fee for Nora every week, regular as clockwork. I'm not going to sully that agreement, so you keep your little sweetener. Save your tips for the whores."

Frank checked his monitoring bracelet. Blimey. Seph had meant it when she said she had topped up

THOSE OF THE LIGHT

his balance.

"Fifty thousand."

"What?" The man spluttered on his whisky.

"Fifty thousand credits for one minute of Nora's time. She'll confirm I am who I say I am. If not, you can chuck me out into the street."

The man's face turned pale and sweaty with excitement. He leaned low against the bar, conspiratorially, and glanced towards Perval, still bickering with the bouncers.

"Payment up front," he whispered, holding out his wrist.

Frank transferred the money and the deal was done.

"Jeez. Either you are who you say you are or you're a madman, buddy. Here." He placed a tall, chilled glass of beer on the bar. "On the house. Give me a minute and I'll take you a different way, through the back of the bar and the kitchen, to

Nora's dressing room. Avoid..." He stole a glance towards Perval. "Avoid any rumours."

Frank nodded, already enjoying his pint. He needed it, to calm the nervous butterflies now fluttering in his stomach. This was it.

A few minutes passed until, true to his word, the guy returned and gestured Frank through the bar into the staff only zone beyond. They walked through the kitchen into a hallway lined with doors, most of them open as girls moved between them, fixing up each other's hair and applying make-up. One door was closed, in the very centre.

The boss man knocked gently and cracked it open, poking his head inside.

"I brought the guy, hun. Let me know which gutter you want me to throw him into once you've seen it's not him." He held the door open and stepped to one side, his hand directing Frank to enter.

"The one the regulars use as a urinal, please, Willy," Nora said, looking at her dressing-gowned reflection in the mirror as she brushed her hair. She placed the brush on the table and turned. "If he's my husband, I'll eat his... Frank!" Her eyes shot open wide and filled with tears as she stared at him, silenced, stunned.

"As long as it's been, it's probably not the place and time for that, love," Frank teased, his voice cracking. "Did I really just say that? I take it back."

Nora giggled as joyful tears fell down her face.

"I can't believe it," she said, as she rushed into his arms, slamming herself against his chest in the tightest hug, before rising on her toes and kissing every inch of his face. She reached a hand up and stroked his hair. "Oh, sweetie, are you ok? How long since you crossed over? You seem a little frazzled, though I must admit your devastatingly handsome. I don't remember you being this good looking in your twenties."

"Oh yes, I was always a dish. And you don't look a day older than eighty-eight." He received an affectionate shove for his insolence.

"But really, baby, are you ok? I've missed you so much but at least I knew I might someday see you again. I can't imagine what the last few years have been like for you, thinking I was gone forever."

"They were...they were..." Something broke inside of him as every agonised moment of grief crumbled away, vanishing, like an hourglass flipped over. It was some minutes before he could compose himself and speak. "But it doesn't matter now. I got my darling, my Nora." Frank kissed her with all his built-up love and desire, certain it was the best moment of his life.

Nora jumped in his arms as the door of her dressing room slammed against the wall.

"I think you'll find she's *my* Nora," a raging,

bloody-nosed Perval said, an angry smirk on his face. "You'll get your hands off my fiancée."

"How did you get back here?" the boss said, stepping in between Perval, and Nora and Frank.

"You're the one who has some explaining to do, Willy," Perval said. "Why the hell…"

"I'm not his fiancée," Nora whispered to Frank as the two men argued. "I didn't say yes. I just didn't say no because otherwise I'd have had to… I'd…"

He held her head to his chest. "I know, Nora, I know. You had to. I'm glad you did. It was smart, but then you always were the clever one in our relationship, much cleverer than me."

"Well, it's not like that's hard."

"Cheeky mare."

"I knew I had to keep up the act, that it would only be a matter of time before you passed over. I knew you'd find me."

"Always. And you kept singing our song. I

watched you out front, but you didn't see me."

"Yes, I did. Not in the room, of course, but in my mind. Always in my mind. Who do you think I was singing to?"

The kerfuffle between Perval and Willy intensified as they both shoved and shouted. The two bodyguards from the doorway near the stage appeared and broke them apart, sweaty and out of breath.

"Sorry, boss," one of the bodyguards said. "He slipped past us. We managed to grab him but he got away."

"Look," Willy said, red-faced but holding up hands of peace. "We've got a bit of a situation here. I get it, you're angry. You've spent a lot of money on Nora. But then you always knew this could happen, she's always said she was waiting for Frank. So, here's what I propose. No one has to walk away from this empty-handed. If Frank wants his wife back, then he should refund everything Perval has paid for Nora with interest. The same goes for the price I paid for her. That way, we guys make a little money, the lovebirds are reunited, everyone's happy. What do you say?"

Nora rolled her eyes. "Always the businessman, Willy."

"You know it, baby."

It was a nifty solution, but Frank knew Perval would never go for it even before he looked at him. He knew because he understood what it was to love Nora. Perval would give everything he had to have her, as Frank would. He turned to him, expecting to see outrage, fury. Instead, Perval's eyes glinted with perverse joy.

"No deal, I'm afraid. Like I said, Nora's mine." He reached into his pocket and pulled out a document. "I got the license rushed through this morning, now I work directly for Caligo."

"Woah," Willy said, turning to Nora. "I'm sorry, hun, but I'm not messing with royal business. If he really does have those connections, you'd better do as he says."

"I have connections, too. How else do you think I got all those credits? There can be more where that came from, I'm sure. I not only work for Princess Persephone, but I'm her friend. Her equal. Is that true of you and your master, shit stain?"

"Frank!" Nora admonished. "Well, I suppose it suits him. He does have the personality of a week-old skid mark."

"That's not a nice thing to say about your future husband," Perval spat. "But I can teach you some manners later. Legally, you are mine and there is nothing you can do about it."

Frank felt Nora's grip on him tighten and his blood pounded a rageful rhythm in his ears.

"But she's my wife!"

"Not down here," Perval said with a smug chuckle. "Marriage is null and void as soon as surds descend. New marriages have to be approved and now mine has. Did you think you could just slip away from the Barn and take her?"

"I'll kill you!" Frank ran at Perval, forcing him into the hallway and slamming him against the wall. He punched like his fists didn't belong to him, unable to stop until several hands grabbed him and pulled him away, struggling, resisting. He wriggled free enough to avoid being knocked out cold when the guards that someone had called subdued him with their pulse batons, his sidestep meaning he missed the worst of it, but he was brought to his knees, nonetheless.

He watched as Nora struggled in Perval's grip, wanting to laugh and cry when she kicked him in the nuts and got a slap across the face in return. The guards were on Perval's side the moment he showed them the license. Once Willy explained everything to the guards, they shook Perval's hand as they accompanied him and Nora away. Away from Frank.

"Nora…"

He struggled to his feet and followed as fast as his cramping legs would allow, wobbling with every step.

"Let her go, man," Willy shouted after him. "There's nothing you can do."

"Nora!"

By the time Frank made it into the street, Perval and his guard escort had already dragged her deep into the crowd.

"Frank!"

As his legs gave way, footsteps rushed towards him, and he felt hands grab him once more. Only this time, it was Rockford and his men, catching him as he fell.

"Please, Rockford," Frank begged, nodding in Nora's direction. "Please, stop them."

"Get after them," Rockford barked at his men, who ran off as instructed. "Easy, Frank, easy."

He was exhausted, his body trembling with pain and fear, the ache in his heart returning. When he heard the defeat in the soldiers' slow return, he didn't need to look up to understand.

"I'm sorry, Frank." Rockford said. "She's gone."

NICOLA CURRIE

11

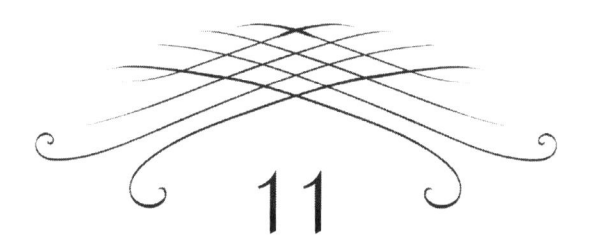

Frank recovered on his bed at the palace, his legs still tremoring and jolting every so often, as he tried to figure out how he would find Nora now. Tulip scratched and squeaked in her cage, pining for Cragor.

"I know how you feel, girl. I know how you feel."

He had been so close. Nora was alive. That was what mattered, but she could be anywhere. And the thought of Perval's hands on her…he forced the idea away. He had to be smart, but he couldn't see an answer. How would Seph react when he told her he could no longer help her and the other Light Seekers? He wouldn't think about trying to escape to the surface until Nora was safely by his side, once and for all. And what did that mean for Frank? Would he be sent back to the Barn, unable to travel, unable to search for her? And what did it mean for Cragor, Tilourik, and his brother, if he could no longer help them either? What kind of friend did that make him?

He couldn't rest, despite the late hour, not with so many *what ifs* and *hows* buzzing in his head. If anyone had answers, it would be Seph. He rose to his feet as soon as the sore muscles in his legs would allow and stepped into the corridor.

The palace was silent now. Porters slept on chaise lounges in each hallway and room, but otherwise no one could be seen or heard. At least, not until he had climbed up the grand staircase to

Seph's apartment and could hear raised voices coming from within.

"Why are you being so difficult, Persephone?" a woman's voice said. "So disobedient? And the ingratitude! King Gehen is the most powerful man in the planet. Your match with him will secure greater prosperity for all of Sub-Europa. He is the richest of Kings too. You'll want for nothing."

"Except sunlight," Seph growled. "Except freedom."

Frank peered through a crack in the door. Seph stood with arms folded, like a defiant teenager, in front of a tall, elegant woman dressed in burgundy silk. It matched her eyes, a deep purple red, an equal mix of the shades of Seph's eyes and her brother's. Their purple lost all their mystery and majesty when muddied with Caligo's bloody shade, and they did not sparkle as Seph's did either. No sympathy or kindness resided there. Her hair a bloody brown too, its waves wrapped up around the sides of a golden diadem, coiled like pythons around its shining band as though clinging to the power it gave.

Queen Gaeatrix, Seph's mother, Frank assumed.

"Not this again." Queen Gaeatrix sighed. "It's not your fault, I suppose. I indulged you with your childish fantasies of the surface because I was certain you would grow out of them, as any daughter blessed with an ounce of sense would. All the more reason you have need of Gehen. When you are with him in the dark deep places of the earth and have all the treasures of the planet's heart in your hands, you'll forget your silly dreams of the sun."

"But I've never seen it," Seph said, in a small voice that should have stirred any loving mother. "Not once. You promised. You've always promised."

"And I intended to keep my promise. I saw no harm in allowing you to take a discreet one-off trip to the surface before you wed, as a royal privilege. But King Gehen forbade such an outing when he agreed the terms of your marriage to him with your father before he passed. He thinks you the rarest of beauties and would maintain your perfection. He does not wish for your cream skin to be touched by the sun. You are to be the jewel in his crown. And think of your eyes. They must adjust to the shadows when you descend. They have no need of blinding light."

"And that is what *you* wish for your only daughter? Endless darkness?"

"I wish I had no daughter at all than have one so selfish and spoilt. I am your Mother and your Queen. You will obey me. Whether you like it or not."

Before Frank had a chance to move or hide, Gaeatrix strode to the door and flung it open. She jumped back in shock when she found him on the other side of it, her eyes narrowing as she raised her voice in furious alarm.

"Guards! An assassin, creeping outside the Princess's chamber. Who are you that has the gall to linger here?"

He heard the clamour of armoured footsteps rushing towards them. Panicking, he looked over the Queen's shoulder into the room beyond. Seph mouthed the word *Bow*. Frank instantly fell into character.

"Forgive me, your most noble majesty." He bent forward, slinging one arm across his middle. "I did not mean to intrude. I came to discuss the designs for the new fountain at the Princess's command."

"This is our new Chief of the Gardens, Mama," Seph said, brushing tears from her eyes. "I said I would build the fountain in King Gehen's honour. You will see I am not entirely disobedient."

Gaeatrix's eyes were still narrowed as she

examined him with a look of distaste, but she waved away the soldiers. Frank rose from his bow as they clanked back to their stations.

"This is a strange hour for such business, but I will allow it. King Gehen must be astonished and enthralled. Your fountain will be a public declaration of your love, Persephone. Perform this duty well and our little squabbles will be at an end."

"Yes, Mama."

"Good girl," she said, walking to the stairs. "Though you mustn't invite your slaves to your chamber next time. It is most unbecoming."

When she was gone, Frank joined Seph in her apartment. She headed for the side table, though tonight wine didn't seem to cut it. She poured three fingers of clear liquor apiece into two glass tumblers.

"Pure crystal vodka," she said with a cough, after knocking it back. "I was saving it for the surface, but what's the point? I'm a fool for thinking I'd ever make it. Here, I bet you could use one too."

He took the glass but didn't drink it. Now he understood the fate that awaited Seph, the full weight of his betrayal sat heavily upon him. "Seph, I—"

"It's okay, Rockford filled me in and I'm smart enough to put two and two together. You can't help the LSR reach the surface while Nora's still lost somewhere here below. Does that about sum it up?"

Frank nodded. He needed a drink after all and swallowed it straight. The surprising coolness of it helped calm his anxious mind.

"Good stuff, huh?" Seph said with a sad smile. "Perfect for the night you realise your dreams will never come true. When Rockford told me about Nora and I understood what it meant, I tried one last time to ask my mother if she could at least let me visit the surface, just once. It might have been enough to sneak the other members of the LSR out, if nothing else. I should have known not to appeal to her better nature. She doesn't have one."

"Are things really so hopeless without me as part of the plan? There must be another option worth trying. What have you got to lose?"

"I agree with you," Seph said, downing a second glass. "If it were just me, I'd take any and every risk I needed to. But it's not. I can't make a run for it on my own. That would betray the others, after so many years of promises. And I can't take them with me without a plan that has some chance of working. I'd be leading them to certain death. I can't do that, even if it means giving up the sun."

"Don't you think you should let them decide how much they want to risk? Wendamel seems like a game old girl."

"More than you know," Seph laughed. "She once seduced a barrier guard a hundred years her junior so we could access a disused route we thought might lead to the surface. It was a whole kind of stern headmistress and naughty schoolboy situation, I believe, but I didn't ask for the gory details. We were wrong about the route but it put a smile on her face, the saucy little minx." Seph's smile fell away and her gaze dropped to the bottom of her glass. "Can you imagine it? To live as long as she has here below? I'd rather die than have another three hundred years down here. Hell, another ten."

"Anyway…" Seph sat on the edge of her bed, cupping her glass with both hands and staring into it as though wishing it were a crystal ball. "At least it means I can save Cragor. I'll agree to marry Gehen and visit my brother in the morning to ask him to give me Cragor as a wedding gift, to be my household slave. And that other guy, Tilourik? His brother too. Crag will never forgive me, but I'll have to live with that after all. He'll never go hungry again. That's something."

Frank didn't know what to say. He knew Cragor would never stand for it, but what else could Seph do?

Seph wandered over to one of her many wardrobes. A long dress of black lace with a huge train, puffy shoulders, and a very revealing peephole where the wearer's cleavage would be, hung above one of them. She ran her fingers over it, tentatively, as though stroking a poisonous snake.

"Disgusting, isn't it? One of Gehen's emissaries brought it with him. Gehen has a very specific idea of what he wants. Who he wants. And I have to spend the rest of my life pretending to fit into that part. I suppose that's nothing new. But we were so close!" Seph swiped the dress to one side with an angry smack, knocking it off its peg. "If only we knew how to find Perval. We'd have a chance to find Nora and our shot at the surface. I already sent

Rupert to look into him at the Barn—he's worked for the Safety Inspection Office for years now, which helped us narrow down our escape options—and all he could find out was that Perval quit the Barn minutes after you left. The Head Foreman had no idea where he went. It could take months to figure out where he is, by which time I'll be Persephone, Queen of Darkness."

"Yeah, Perval said he worked for your brother again now, that's how he got the marriage license. Could we find an address through the records office or—"

Out of nowhere, Seph slapped him across the face. The vodka had numbed him somewhat, but it still stung. A second later, she grabbed him in a tight hug.

"You're a fucking idiot, Frank," Seph said. "But you're going to get us all out of here so I forgive you."

"Huh?" he said, dizzy from a cocktail of vodka and confusion. "What just happened? Did I miss something?"

"I said you're a fucking idiot. Did you not think it might be helpful to mention that the man who has your wife is now working for my brother, seeing as I know where my brother lives? If Perval is his lackey again, he'll be there, keeping Nora nearby. You need to give me the vital information, kid."

"Sorry, I thought Rockford would have told…" Come to think of it, he wasn't sure he'd mentioned Perval's change in job status to Rockford, either. In his electrified, rebroken distress, he'd failed to see the significance. Seph's slap hadn't been hard enough. He had almost let everything slip away.

"I'm a fucking idiot," Frank said.

"Yep!" Seph said, grinning from ear to ear now. "Soon you get to be the hero though. My brother's palace is on the edge of the pit works nearest to this city. If Nora is there with Perval, that means everyone we need to rescue is in one place. This is it. We get our girl and guys and go—surface or bust!"

"Can we move that fast? Do you have everything prepared?"

Excited, Seph paced to and fro, her drinking glass discarded.

"Things are a little scrappy, but I won't be able to sleep tonight, anyway. I feel it, it's now or never." Before he could turn away or blush, Seph stepped out of the dress she was wearing until she stood in nothing but her underwear.

"You can stop staring, perv."

"You can stop flashing me, hussy."

"Touché." Seph pulled on her black overalls and leather jacket. "I'm calling in on Wend, Lil, and Rupert. They can get everyone else ready. Get a good night's sleep. With any luck, we'll be rising to the surface by this time tomorrow and you'll need to be in the best shape you can be if you're going to watch over us throughout the ascent and still be sane when we reach the top. Come back here when you've had a solid eight hours and a big breakfast. I mean it. Go to bed."

"Yes, Mum," Frank mocked.

Seph didn't hear him. She'd already rushed out of the room and down the stairs without another word.

Nerves, excitement, and the aftereffects of the crystal vodka gurgled in his belly as Frank stepped out onto Seph's balcony and looked at the neon-lit city beyond. He hoped it would be the last time he saw it.

"I'm coming, darling," he said to Nora, wherever she was in the night.

NICOLA CURRIE

12

Despite Seph's strict instructions, Frank did not fall asleep until the early hours of the next day. Tulip was racing in her wheel when he returned to his room, as if pointing out the other problem he had to solve. What was he going to do with Tulip?

When he eventually slept, hamsters running through his dreams, he slept hard and didn't awake until mid-morning. After breakfast, he snuck a knife from the buffet table and asked one of the kitchen staff for a packed lunch so he could work undisturbed in the garden. When he got back to his room, he threw the sandwiches he had been given into the bin, more interested in the tub that had contained them. It wasn't a perfect solution, but with a few holes stabbed into the plastic and a little of her bedding added, it would provide a temporary, and more importantly portable, home for Tulip until they reached the surface.

Frank picked her up and put her inside. He got a nip on his finger for the cheek of waking her, but she soon relaxed and curled up back to sleep. He placed this most precious of lunch boxes in a backpack he found in his wardrobe, surrounding Tulip's new carrier with towels from the bathroom to protect her from any jolt or jostle. He left it unzipped at the top so air could flow and pulled the straps over his shoulders. There was nothing he needed to take for himself. Everything he and Nora could want waited in the life above.

When he returned to Seph's apartment, he found her downing drinks again, only this time vast quantities of coffee. She had dark circles under her eyes but was jittery with energy.

"Perfect timing," she said, tightening her boots. "We're all set. The LSR have agreed on our best shot at a functioning ascension tunnel within the vicinity of the Pit. Should anyone ask, our cover story is that I'm visiting my brother to discuss my upcoming wedding and I'm taking you to look at the fountain in his palace garden for inspiration. I'll keep Caligo distracted inside while you and Rockford search for Nora, Cragor, Tilourik, and his brother. The rest of the LSR are coming through the hidden wellways and will meet us not far from the tunnel. We leave no one behind. We all make it, or none of us do. Shit, I didn't think about Tulip."

"Way ahead of you," Frank said, twisting and pointing to the backpack. "I couldn't go without this fluffy bundle of attitude."

"Good, because this not so fluffy bundle of attitude thinks we need to get a move on. I hope you got your rest, sleepyhead, now let's go."

Rockford met them in the courtyard. It struck Frank as strange that neither Rockford nor Seph carried anything with them, that they were leaving behind the life they knew yet taking nothing of it with them. But perhaps it wasn't so strange. Why take mementos from a life you wished to forget?

"Wait a second," Seph said.

They turned into a secluded recess in a corner of the courtyard, hidden by a jagged black tree that had a trunk like a stalagmite. The small space behind must have served as a tiny respite for Seph in her younger days, doodles and scribblings and signatures etched into the jewelled bricks. She removed a wedge of topaz and pulled out a drawstring bag, tipping the contents into her hand.

"I've been collecting stray rocks and chippings from the palace walls over the years, to give us a little something to get started with above. I think it's worth a bit up there. It should buy us some food at least."

"I'd say so," Frank said, once he had wrestled his eyebrows down from the top of his forehead. Seph had jewels big enough and shiny enough to fund several generations. "I think it'll do." He noticed another chunk had cracked off from a large brick of glorious sapphire. "Look, there's one there too."

"Keep it," Seph said with a smirk, snatching it up and throwing it to him. "Something to remember this place by."

"A keepsake…sure…" He slipped the stone into his pocket, certain he could get at least twenty grand for it from the jewellers on his old high street, maybe more, if its size and shine were anything to go by.

Seph's (and her grandkids') wealth secured, they walked around the palace to a side gate that led onto a platform, with a track that disappeared along the palace's own private tunnel. A single golden carriage waited for them.

The first part of their journey was punctuated every few minutes by another barrier, with the same guarded checkpoints and intense lights Frank had seen when he'd travelled with Seph before. Gradually they became less frequent, until they travelled in darkness in a tunnel that curved downwards for so long, Frank wondered how much lower it was possible to go.

"How far below are we exactly?"

"Not far when you compare it to the deeper cultures, like Gehen and his people. To them, I'm practically a surd. That's how they would have seen me too, if Mother had had her way and made me marry him. I don't understand why she thinks it a

THOSE OF THE LIGHT

good idea. They don't like us. They never have. Caligo used to tell me horror stories about them, their minds gone mad in their utter darkness. I've heard they tell their own scary tales too, about burning light and those who walk in it."

Frank knew he could never quite feel the same way again if they made it back to the surface. He'd always wonder what was under his feet.

The train levelled out and they emerged into a wide cavern. It was oppressively hot, sweat dripping from Frank's forehead within seconds. There was the offending noise of clanking industry too. On the left side of the train, hundreds of people toiled in some kind of giant refinery or foundry, machinery and pipes covering the ground into the distance. Large groups operated what looked like gigantic industrial pestles slamming into mortar basins the size of lakes. Each was heated from below by ferocious bubbling pools of lava that ran in a network of molten red rivers between each mammoth grinder, and through the crowd of sweltering workers. He watched as one of the machines paused so a stony substance could be added by the truckload into the huge basin, before the endless crush began again.

"I don't understand. What are they making?"

"Other side," Seph said. "The Pit."

Frank gasped. The space to the right of the train was so enormous he could not see the end of it. The thick black greasy horizon of the still sea before him met eventually with the cavern ceiling in his line of sight, continuing out of view for he didn't know how far.

Oil. Vast vast quantities of oil, ready to be delivered to the surface above or piped back into the city.

He saw it now, the pipes that passed beneath the tracks, depositing the liquid juiced from the stony material.

Wait… He was no expert, but even if there was a way to speed up the formation of oil by creating increased heat and pressure, he was pretty sure oil did not come from stone. It came from…

"Dear God!" Frank said, and Seph gave him a grimace in confirmation. He saw what other workers were loading into chippers.

Bones. Human bones.

"It's like everyone always says," she said sadly. "Those condemned to the Pit never make it out."

"But then Cragor…Tilourik…"

She shook her head. "Crag's a good labourer. They'll be put to work first. They only kill those who can't hack it. We got here in time. We have to have."

The track sloped upwards, rising over the expansive field of workers until they were scurrying ants below. And that's how Caligo and his kind see them, Frank thought angrily, as Caligo's dark palace, perched high above on the cliff, came into view.

It was as black as Gaeatrix's home was dazzling, glinting in an obsidian marble that shined as slickly as the ocean of oil beneath it. Smaller than the Queen's estate, its spiked battlements and parapets made it more imposing, as though it spoke of a viciousness residing within.

They stopped in front of the main door. The position of the palace created a natural fortress—the train was the only way to the track below and anywhere else beyond. As Seph and Frank approached the door, Rockford stayed onboard.

"I'll head back down. I'll find your boys. I'm friendly with a few of the guards here, swine that they are."

The interior was all red and black, blood and death, Frank noted as they went inside. The scarred house servant who greeted them wore grey rags and looked at the ground. Red tapestries lined the walls while black candles blazed. The ebony floor was carpeted with crimson rugs and the hides of monstrous ruddy-coloured bears, fangs displayed.

Caligo rose from a high-backed chair of dark wood as they entered his receiving chamber. Another bowed servant scurried away with tear-stained cheeks as he dismissed her with a hand and demanded wine.

"Sister!" Caligo said with open arms. "Mother has sent word of your glorious news. I'm glad you've seen sense and accepted your place. You will serve Gehen and he will serve Sub-Europa in return."

Seph managed a strained smile, but Frank could see the suppressed fury in her eyes.

"I'm so glad you approve, brother, and would welcome your aid in preparing for such an advantageous wedding. In the meantime…"

As she spun her tale about the fountain and his fictitious role in creating it, Frank searched around for any sign of Nora. A balcony overlooked the room, with doors on the upper level beyond, but no one was in sight apart from forlorn servants. They moved silently around the palace, as quiet as a morgue, as though all who found themselves there had long since abandoned hope.

"Of course," Caligo said, when Frank returned his attention to the conversation. His red eyes turned to him and gestured to a door at the back of the room. "That way. Hurry along now. Your betters have much to discuss in private."

Frank did as bid and exited into the hallway beyond. Directly opposite, an open backdoor led into a courtyard. He wasn't interested in the fountain there, of course, but as he tried to turn down a corridor instead, to look for Nora somewhere in the palace's rooms, a servant came towards him. With no choice but to play his part, he stepped outside.

The fountain was grotesque. A statue of a crowned Caligo stood in a warrior pose above a group of minions bowed at his feet. Red water flowed from his gory eyes, turning the pool beneath bloody. If a similar fountain was intended to honour Gehen, Frank feared for Seph if their plan failed.

He couldn't think of that now. He had to find a way inside, to Nora. As he decided to circle around to the front as covertly as he could, the servant previously dismissed in tears stepped out the backdoor, a mop and bucket in hand. Frank paused and pretended to admire the fountain. She stopped beside him, throwing away her mop water on the ground nearby.

"In the maze," she whispered, so quietly he thought at first she might be talking to herself.

"I'm sorry? I don't know what you mean." His confusion was only part pretence.

"Yes, you do," the woman whispered. "She's waiting in the maze." She turned and took her empty bucket inside without a word more.

"Umbra Iubar," he murmured to himself. "Shadow's Radiance." The vicious flower was the only thing of beauty in this place of darkness. A wall of it formed the back edge of the courtyard. Except there was a gap in it, Frank realised, as he approached.

Brilliant. I was thinking this hell hole needed something a bit more on the bitey side.

He breathed in and, positioning himself in the middle of the path, stepped into the flower-lit maze.

It took a few minutes to find the way to the open square at the maze's centre and before he had registered he had, Nora flew into his arms.

"I knew it," she said. "When I overheard Caligo

tell Perval the Princess would be visiting, I knew you were coming for me. How are we going to get out of this? Perval wants to marry me this afternoon and went into the city to make the final arrangements. I tried to escape from here, but I don't have the clearance to use a train and there is no other way out of this sodding palace. Perval will be back any moment."

"Too bad we'll soon be long gone," Frank said, kissing her on the forehead. "Poor Perval. And you'd have made such a lovely couple."

Nora gave him a playful swat in the ribs. "Don't joke about it. I'd jump off the side of the cliff before he could make me go through with it. It's not just that he's vicious and unkind that makes him so repulsive. It's that he's so pathetic. He always needs to strut and act like he's important because underneath it all, I think even he knows he's so…empty. He wanted me as a trophy. He isn't capable of knowing what love is. Every time he tries to touch my arm or hold my hand, I flinch. He's so clammy. When he gets excited, he's like a jittery fish. It's disgusting."

"I'm not so clammy right now, darling," Perval said as he appeared from the bushes. "I've got a pretty good grip, anyway."

Frank and Nora stared into the light of the pulse gun Perval was aiming towards them.

"And don't worry about my excited hands for the moment," he continued. "They'll get well acquainted with you later, babe."

He circled them as they stood in the heart of the maze, pacing slowly, like the threat of a minute hand counting down to a dreaded fate. Frank held Nora tighter. He wouldn't lose her, not again. Not ever again.

"What's the matter, Perval? Never been popular with the ladies, so you have to bully one into marrying you? Maybe just try being less of a dick, mate."

The hatred in his eyes told Frank he had hit a nerve but goading him wasn't his only intention. With Perval distracted by his own rage and insecurity, Frank considered the exits. Perval blocked the way he had come and there was no way to tell whether the other gaps that led off from the centre would take them back to the palace or to a dead end with no hope of escape. As Perval's grip tightened around his gun, Frank slid his hand into his pocket and made a choice.

"Less? Your wife will be getting a whole lot more later," Perval said with his defining smirk. "What a thought for you to die with."

Perval pressed the trigger, but Frank was quicker. Without a second to spare, he grabbed the sapphire from his pocket and let it fly, landing it squarely between Perval's eyes. As the gun went off, the shot askew, he pulled Nora into the gap to the left of the centre, hoping one of its routes led back to the courtyard and they could make it to the train before Perval caught them.

"Argh!" A cry of frustration chased behind as Frank heard footsteps running after them. The gun went off again and he felt an electric buzz whizz past his sprinting foot as they turned a corner.

They ran hand in hand, yanking each other down tunnel after tunnel, the deadly flowers snapping at them, ripping the edges of their clothes. He swung the backpack forward around his other arm and held it against his chest, steadying it as much as he could.

"No, down here," Frank said, pulling Nora away from her route to his when they reached two parallel paths, despite her protestations. He regretted it when the very next turning led to an abrupt dead end, into a small alcove with little room to stand in without being nipped. He scolded himself.

Always listen to the wife.

Another shot crackled in the air. Perval wasn't far behind them. Too late to head back to the path Nora had wanted to take, they could only step out of the alcove and continue along Frank's way, towards the last turn ahead, hoping it led somewhere. It ran straight for a fair bit, then curved to the right, in the direction of the palace. They just might make it…

"Shit!".

Dead end. They had nowhere else to go. In his distraction, he stood too close to the bush and an agile bud leaped out at him, nipping a hand he'd splayed out in frustration. It gave him an idea, the only idea he could think of to save them. "Go back."

"But we'll never make it to the other route," Nora said, as the footsteps got closer, a hedge away. "We'll barely reach—"

"The alcove," Frank said, glancing at Nora as they ran, seeing understanding bloom in her eyes.

They both knew what they had to do.

They stepped into the alcove's shadow a mere moment before Perval turned onto the path it connected to.

"You're both fucked, you hear me," Perval roared as he rushed in their direction. "You're both— Arghhhhh!"

As Perval passed the alcove, Frank and Nora threw themselves forwards, their hands overlapping, one on top of the other, as they pushed him backwards. The flowers did not hesitate. As soon as Perval hit the hedge, they lunged, sinking their fangs into him like grapples seizing a captured ship.

"Argh! Help! Hel—" Perval screamed. The flowers pulled together and dragged him into the bush until he was a part of it, vanishing behind their radiance and unable to cry out any longer. Several metres of the hedge wall flushed pink as, finally,

THOSE OF THE LIGHT

something wanted him.

Maybe they should have paused and considered the life they had taken, Frank thought as they walked back to the centre and down the pathway they knew led to the courtyard. But he cared too much about the life that might now lie ahead, and he would never forgive the monster of a man who had almost taken that from him, who had almost taken the person who gave his life light.

Even if he was now nothing more than plant food.

When they reached the courtyard, Rockford was waiting.

"Nice to meet you, Miss," he said to Nora, with a bow. "I'll take you to the train." She followed him, hesitating, still holding on to Frank's hand as she walked away, their arms outstretched.

"It'll just be a moment, I promise," Frank said. "I have to play my part and join the Princess. We'll follow shortly."

Reluctantly, she released his hand and left with Rockford, circling around the side of the palace. Knowing she was in safekeeping, Frank went inside.

Seph was still speaking to Caligo, but now, Cragor, Tilourik, and a third man knelt nearby, a cluster of grey-ragged servants watching over them.

Tilourik was a wreck, his face skinny and sallow, exhaustion weathering every inch of his skin. The equally ruined man next to him could have been his twin. His brother, Frank assumed, the one who had searched the records for him. Cragor was covered in sweat and dirt, and his deadly expression suggested he was very, very hungry. A smile teased the corner of his mouth when they locked eyes, nonetheless. They were all alive. That was what would matter in the long run, when the Pit and those who controlled it were a memory.

"It seems my royal gardener has finished his considerations. I should bid you farewell and thank you for the gifts you have given me. You've been generous, brother," Seph said.

"Have I?" Caligo replied, absent-mindedly contemplating a long steel blade that decorated a part of the wall. "Sweet sister, you have misunderstood me."

He reached up and took the blade, holding it upright and admiring its shine as he walked towards his servants and the men who knelt at their feet. Before Frank realised what was happening, Caligo yanked Cragor's head backwards, the sharp sword held to his neck.

"Wha...what are you doing?" Seph said, the role she played faltering as her face paled. "They're my slaves. You promised you'd gift them to me."

"Yes, well, it's all in the details, isn't it?" Caligo said, relishing his sister's distress. "I meant more in a sacrificial sense. Besides, I can't imagine King Gehen would be pleased to learn you'd smuggled your boyfriend into his realm. Oh, you thought I didn't know? Little sister, please. You aren't the only one who knows things."

Before he had the chance to slide the blade one millimetre along Cragor's throat, Seph flung herself across the room, grabbed onto him, and yanked his sword arm away. Caligo responded with a shove and an angry swipe, the blade drawing a thin river of blood from her shoulder.

He did not get the chance to swing his sword twice.

Cragor exploded towards him, fists clenched into cannonballs. One punch sent the Prince to the floor. Cragor knelt over him, pinning him with his gigantic body, one crushing hand at each temple. As Caligo's eyes streamed, his bloody pools flooding out, Frank thought of the bones he saw in the pit works below and considered what an apt end it was for one who had crushed so many.

"Help me, you fools," Caligo said to his servants. "Don't just stand there!" Some of the forlorn servants moved forwards, obedient despite their poor chances against a man such as Cragor, until one halted the rest with a wave of her arm. The previously tear-stained woman watched as Caligo's skull was squeezed between the pressure of Cragor's hands, without the slightest sparkle of water in her eye. The others stopped and watched with her.

"Wha…doing…stp…urg…graaaaaaaa..."

Caligo's red stare gushed as did his ears, nose, and mouth, until, with an audible crack, he was silent, the blood in his eyes a terror to no one any longer.

"You can stop now, Crag," Frank said gently, laying a hand on his shoulder. "He can't hurt her now."

Time seemed to pause for a few seconds until Cragor finally let go, discarding the Prince for his sister.

"I'm okay," Seph said, fear in her eyes as Cragor came towards her, his fury not yet passed from his face. Seph looked like she wasn't sure if Cragor would kill her too, now he knew who she was, or...

Cragor pulled Seph into his arms and kissed her passionately, like they were the only ones in the room.

Really like they were the only ones in the room.

"I know you're hungry, mate," Frank said. "But do you have to eat her face?"

Once they had resurfaced, there was barely time to check Seph's shoulder before the servant woman pushed them all out of the door.

"Go!" she said. "We'll take care of him and then we're getting out of here. The Chief Housekeeper's clearance will get us as far as it can and then I'm escaping back to Sub-Afrique, if I can make it."

"Thank you," Frank said. "You saved us, all of us."

"Go!"

Nora smiled as they boarded the train, her eyes widening as she saw the shock on their faces, the blood on Cragor's hands. "What happened?"

"Oh, just another arsehole and another gory death," Frank said. "Nothing unusual. Now shall we get the fuck out of here?"

The train sped away. When it stopped next, there was only one way they were going.

Up.

NICOLA CURRIE

13

"Ooh, sandwiches!" Cragor said, when he reached into the backpack Frank passed to him.

"Not quite," Frank said.

As the plastic box was opened, Tulip stood up on her back legs, stretching up towards Cragor as soon as she realised it was him.

"My angel!" Cragor held out his hand and Tulip stepped onto it, climbing up his arm and settling on his shoulder. "I've missed you so much."

"What about me? Did you miss me?" Frank

asked, yet to even get a hello.

"Of course," Cragor said. "But nowhere near as much."

"Nice to know I still rank just behind a hamster in your affections, Crag."

"Well, not quite. It's Seph, Tulip, the guys that give me extra portions in the Barn canteen, then you."

Nora laughed. As the train carried them towards their final and greatest challenge, nervous and jovial introductions lightened their journey.

"I'm sorry I got you both into this," Frank said to Tilourik and his brother, Rillarook. "Especially because you were trying to help me."

"It's okay," Rillarook said through a yawn. "We wouldn't be headed for the surface if it wasn't for you. And man, I'm looking forward to the trip. I want to sleep for a week."

The train stopped. It had exited a tunnel into a

small, bare cavern. It was the middle of nowhere, with nothing nearby except a crowd of people. Lillibet, Rupert, Wendamel, and twenty others were waiting for them.

"We have to walk the rest of the way," Seph explained, as they stepped out of the carriage. "The trainway that transported goods to the ascension tunnel we're heading for collapsed years ago. That's why it's not used anymore, we think. We're certain it works. Right, Lil?"

"Indubitably," Lillibet nodded. "Everything is set. We have gathered the provisions and medicaments." She pointed to a large backpack carried by the black-eyed, spiky-haired guy.

"Then this is it. Last chance for anyone who wants to back out," Seph said. "No? Then let's do this. Torches!"

Each member of the LSR turned on a battery powered torch, except Lillibet and Rupert, who had antique paraffin lanterns.

"Lillibet's learned the route by heart from the plans she stole," Seph continued. "Lead the way, Lil."

There was a gap in the rock at the back, big enough for them to squeeze through one by one. The passages beyond were narrow in places, tight to get through even in single file. At one point, they had to bend so low it was easier to crawl, and Frank felt himself sweating, panicking. Just as he started to hyperventilate, the passage ended, and they stepped into a cavern that was otherwise entirely enclosed. The rubble of an old guardhouse covered what would have been the tunnel out, the end of the abandoned train track poking up from beneath the crumbled rock.

When he looked up his mouth dropped open in awe. A perfect circle was cut into the rock above in the centre of the cavern, the space within hollowed upwards for a distance he could not fathom, its sides lined with metal as far as he could see. An endless vertical tunnel of darkness. About to swallow him whole.

Beneath it, a circular platform was attached to a circular dock, grasped by metallic arms. It was the same set up as the one he had arrived on. It connected to a conveyor belt on the right side, where further platforms waited, another fifteen lined up.

"I never got involved in the mechanics," Seph said to Frank and the small group that had come from the Pit with him, as the rest of the LSR hugged each other, prayed, and exchanged *I wish you sunlight*s. "I tried, but Mother told the Lead Technician for the ascension tunnel at the arrival hospital I was not to do work that was too menial, if I insisted on volunteering. Not becoming of a princess, apparently. I observed as much as I could.

When one platform rises into the shaft, the conveyor belt moves the next one onto the dock. We'll have to load people platform by platform, two per platform. We're lucky. There are just enough to fit everyone. And you two are first."

Wendamel had wandered over as Seph gave her explanation. She looked at Frank with her cheeky lopsided smile.

"Take your clothes off," she said.

"What you and I had was very special," Frank joked. "But the wife might have something to say about us taking things any further."

Wendamel scowled and said nothing.

"No, she means it this time," Seph said. "Strip to your underwear, both of you."

Nora shrugged and whipped off her shirt without hesitation. Frank was momentarily distracted.

"Damn, baby."

Nora smiled for half a second, then put on her

bossy face.

"Get'em off, sweet cheeks."

Seph smirked at him as he pulled off his trousers and didn't have to say it. He knew exactly what she was thinking. *Cute butt.*

He'd never noticed he had a cute butt before all of this. Then again, how could he? *Is that a thing, arse modelling?* He'd need to find a new career when they got to the surface…

"Puny little pipsqueak," Cragor teased when Frank pulled off his shirt and flexed his biceps.

When they were down to their underwear, the spiky-haired guy slung his backpack at Seph's feet. She opened it and rummaged, pulling out foil packages connected to long tubes.

"We need to give you the greatest chance of staying in the best shape you can if we're relying on you to wake us when we get to the surface. We're going to attach these survival rations under your clothes. They're not particularly palatable, I'm afraid, and you'll have to be sparing, but it will keep your fluid and nutrients topped up enough to make sure you don't die from dehydration and weakness."

When the foil rations had been tied to their arms and their legs, Seph pulled out fresh clothes: T-shirts with cargo trousers and jackets, both covered in pockets.

"There's a red flare gun in your right lower leg pocket. Use it if the platform stops for any reason. There's a green dart gun in your left lower leg pocket. I'll be on the platform beneath you. Do not deviate from the plan unless you have to but, I lead the LSR, so if we must make changes, I make the decisions. The platforms are not flush with the sides. There's a nine-inch gap all the way around. If you need to wake me, lean over and shoot me in the torso with the dart gun. Do not, I repeat, *do not* confuse the *red* flare gun and the *green* dart gun. I really don't want to die a fiery death with a flare to the heart. Repeat that back to me."

"If I fancy changing plans, I'm to shoot you in the heart. I can look through the gap around the platform to watch the pretty fireworks as you burn."

Seph and Nora scowled at him. They were both stunning and terrifying.

"Sometimes, Frank, I worry about you. Has he always been like this?"

"Pretty much," Nora teased. "He thinks he's funny. You learn to drown it out after a while."

"Rude," Frank said. "Besides, I'm not a total idiot."

Seph and Nora stared back at him blankly.

"Double rude! I'm *not* a total idiot. Red flare equals brighty lighty, green dart equals wakey wakey, I get it. Shall we move on with things? I'm looking forward to our terrifying flight into darkness."

They pulled on the clothes as Seph explained the rest of the pocket contents. A battery-powered torch to use as needed if the platform stopped. A small wind-up light they could secure to their lapels so they could see each other easily on their platform. A bottle of pills was the last thing she gave them, to put in Frank's top pocket.

"What are those?"

Seph grimaced. "If the platforms get stuck part of the way up, there is unlikely to be any way to escape. Every member of the LSR will starve to death, but at least we won't be awake to suffer. You will, though. If the worst happens, these pills will give you a merciful end."

The pills terrified Frank, but he clutched them close, nonetheless.

"I have prepared the ingenious magnetic levitation device for departure," Lillibet said from a control module next to the conveyor belt. The

THOSE OF THE LIGHT

metallic arms had released the platform, which hovered some inches now above the dock.

"This is it," Seph said.

"You and Cragor are right behind them," Rockford said. "You should sedate yourselves now. It may take some minutes to work. I'm to go last, with Wendamel. We'll make sure everyone else is boarded safely. Lillibet has shown me how to release the final platform with a delay, so we have time to climb aboard."

Seph and Cragor swallowed a different kind of pill as Frank and Nora climbed onto the platform. As he lay back, Frank saw Cragor crush a tiny section off a pill and feed it to Tulip on his finger, concern on his face, careful not to give her too much. She settled happily in his pocket, against his chest.

"Cragor. You really are a sweetheaRRRRRRRRRRRRR…"

Nora was silent as they shot up with a loud whoosh into black, but Frank screamed for a good ten minutes. The speed of their rushing ascent pinned them to the platform, but Nora reached out and stroked his arm until he calmed as much as he could in such circumstances.

With effort, they turned towards each other in the darkness, kissing, cradling each other's heads, feeling each other's beating hearts. As minutes or hours or days passed, they lay like that, sometimes using their wind-up lights to see nothing but each other's faces, their love for each other in each other's eyes.

At times, Frank forgot where they were. They could already be dead, their souls drifting in space, together forever. He was okay with that.

But they were alive and reunited, he knew, as they urged each other to sip on their rations every now and then.

Sometimes he dreamed of Nora in the sunlight—their tired dawn walks after all night at the dance hall; the light through the stained glass that had illuminated the back of the church as Nora had walked down the aisle towards him, a radiant angel; the glinting sea as they watched their children play along the shore near their beach house, Nora's chestnut hair shining in the sun.

Was he there, or here, with her in the darkness? It made little difference. She was with him. Then he would remember where they were, why, how, and felt so lucky to have his second life with her he would cry.

At some point, after uncountable days, as they gazed at each other after a tiny meal, their senses together in the present, the unexpected happened. The platform slowed to a halt as the deafening whoosh fell silent.

"What's happened?" Nora asked, voice cracking

from under-use.

"I'm not sure," Frank said huskily. He sat up and regretted it. Weak and dizzy, his head spun. He finished his last ration packet, but it was a while after until he felt steady. When he did, he reached down into the pocket on his right leg.

"Red gun," he said. "Brighty lighty". He raised it upwards and fired. For half a second, he was comforted to see the huge space above them, the red light relieving them from the suffocating darkness. But as his eyes adjusted and he saw what was there, his heart sunk.

A crisscross of thick beams blocked off the rest of the way ahead. Fluorescent barrier tape had been wrapped around them, highlighting the exit's disuse. Two hundred metres further up, the shaft ended with a large metal hatch bolted shut to what lay beyond. The surface. They were close.

"Frank, over there," Nora said. "The edge of the

platform."

Frank turned and looked to his left, past Nora. A ladder was attached to the side of the tunnel just above them. His eyes followed where it led. Another tunnel was bored horizontally into the rock, six or seven metres up, continuing to the left. A rusty docking station stood next to its entrance, its conveyor belt disappearing down this new path.

"It must be a maintenance tunnel or something," Nora said. "Maybe it leads somewhere. We should wake the others."

"At least Seph," Frank agreed. "She's the one in charge."

He took the torch from his pocket and shone it over the gap at the edge of the platform.

Seph lay next to Cragor, unconscious.

He gripped the gun and aimed it below.

"Frank!" Nora shouted.

"What? Why are you yelling? I could have

misfired."

"Wrong gun."

Quietly, casually, Frank put the red gun back into his right leg pocket and removed the green dart gun from his left leg pocket instead.

"Don't tell Seph. At worst, she'd murder me. At best she would think I'm an idiot for the rest of her life."

"I think she already does, love, and I think she's half right. Try not to shoot her in the eye, dear."

Nora held the torch as he aimed. It wasn't a bad shot, despite his slip up, and the dart lodged in Seph's stomach. After a few minutes, she stirred.

"Fran... Nor..." she said sleepily, rubbing her eyes. "Wha...happen?"

By the time Frank had explained the obstruction ahead and the option of the tunnel to the side, she was fully awake.

"What choice do we have? Get up there and see

THOSE OF THE LIGHT

if you can get us docked." She reached into her pocket and pulled out her own green gun. "I'll wake up Crag and the others on the platform below ours. They'll wake the ones beneath them with their own dart guns. Etcetera, etcetera. Try to see if there's anything up there that explains why they blocked this way up. I don't like it. Something doesn't feel right."

The ladder was embedded firmly into the rock, but Frank wobbled as he climbed, his energy still low. He pulled Nora up as she crested the top behind him.

They stepped into what did indeed look like a maintenance tunnel. A couple of hardhats gathered dust on hooks attached to the wall near the entrance. An abandoned yellow safety jacket lay crumpled on the pathway next to the conveyor belt a little further in.

The tunnel curved away out of sight around a

corner, but there were two rooms to the side of it. The first was a very disgusting bathroom, but it was the second that made Frank sick to his stomach.

It was a simple office—a desk, a kettle, schematics taped to the wall.

But there was blood. So much old, congealed blood. The man slumped in the chair at the desk had long since bled out, his ragged stump of a leg rotting with the rest of him.

"What the hell happened here?" Nora asked.

"I have no clue. But it looks like it's been a while, whatever it was."

"Do you think it's safe now?"

He wasn't sure and didn't want to be the one to decide. They headed back to the entrance and found the control module next to the docking station. Mercifully, it seemed a more basic version than the one he had glimpsed far below. It had only one control, a lever. It was centred in the middle of its track, by a label that said 'Hold'. If he pushed the lever up, it would align with a setting that said 'Release'. Even Frank was smart enough to realise that might not be a good idea. If the platforms were released from their stalled position, he was pretty sure that would mean the LSR would rush up to a very slammy death against the metal beams above. Instead, he slid the lever down to 'Dock' and their platform rose to the docking station, automatically shifting to the conveyor belt a few moments later when he didn't return the lever to 'Hold'. With 'Dock' still selected, Seph and Cragor's platform rose next. He moved the lever back to the middle when they reached him.

"A demon beetle?" Cragor suggested when Frank and Nora had led them to the bloody room. "I tackled one once at the Barn during an infestation. Damn near took *my* leg off."

"Maybe, but I think it's long gone," Seph said.

"Why do you say that?" Nora had been looking over her shoulder every few seconds since they found the body. "Can you be sure?"

"Because it didn't eat the rest of him. We have to go on, anyway, so let's think positive."

Frank and Nora docked the remaining platforms and explained the situation to the others as Seph and Cragor went ahead to explore. They returned a short while later.

"Come on, everyone," Seph said, face glimmering with excitement in the torchlight. "It's clear and leads upwards, to the surface, I think. We're almost there!"

They followed the curve of the tunnel. Sure enough, it led upwards.

"What's that?" Wendamel said, as they entered a long straight section, rising steeply. "Up there. That…glimmer…that…"

"Sunlight!" Seph, Rockford, and several others

yelled at once. They rushed up the underground hill towards the sunlight that shone down from the surface.

"Wait," Frank called after them. He hadn't felt right for a while now, as they walked along. There was something wrong that he couldn't put his finger on.

But it was louder now. As he saw a patch of old dried blood on the ground below, he realised, as he heard it again, coming from inside the rock on one side of the tunnel.

A slithering.

"Seph, stop!"

Rock exploded as a humungous caenosa worm burst through a crack in the wall. Its nightmarish teeth sliced through two members of the LSR, shredding them to pieces and sucking them up like spaghetti.

"Bryda! Willian! No!" Seph screamed.

Rock and earth were falling all around them, the ground beneath them shaking as the worm thrashed the full length of its massive bulk. Frank lost hold of Nora's hand in the noise and chaos as he fell to the floor.

"Frank!"

He turned his torch to the sound of Nora's voice and saw the worm's giant jaw open before her.

"Nora!"

As the worm struck, Wendamel leapt from the darkness and shunted Nora aside. Wendamel didn't scream but kicked and punched the beast with everything she had, even as it bit her in two.

"No!"

Frank yanked Nora away but didn't run. He grabbed the biggest rocks he could and started pelting the caenosa with them, knocking out a front fang, drawing blood from its flesh.

As the worm shrieked, others threw rocks, too.

The worm lashed out, becoming confused. When Cragor hit it with a huge, jagged rock that split a nasty gash into its side, gelatinous milk spilled everywhere as it jerked in anger. As stone and earth fell all around them, it retreated back into the crack in the wall. As a boulder hit Frank on the head, the last thing he heard before he lost consciousness was its distant whimper, fading as it slithered away.

NICOLA CURRIE

14

"Frank! Frank!"

He awoke in the suffocating darkness to the sound of his wife crying beside him.

"Nora…"

He tried to reach out to her, but his body was pinned. The collapse of the rock above them had slowed, but he could still feel the trickle of earth falling upon his head. He was buried up to his shoulders. Soon, the tunnel would be filled with it, and he'd suffocate to death after all. A boy again, crushed on the platform. He started to panic.

They all did. By the few random streams of torchlight that remained above the rubble, Frank could see the others struggling to free themselves. He wriggled and freed his arms, but there was no point. No beam of sunlight shone through any longer. The exit had collapsed. They were trapped. No way forward, no way back.

Seph was the first to get herself loose, pulling her legs up and kneeling in the small space that remained of the tunnel above her, trying to ignore the dirt rushing in.

"We have to dig ourselves out," she yelled, as Cragor joined her. "We're so close. We have to dig up!"

Frank fought against the weight of the rubble and lifted himself. He helped Nora and a few others, too. He crawled up next to Cragor. He, and everyone else, followed Seph and dug upwards. But the earth still fell.

"It's filling up faster!" a panicked voice said.

"We're running out of air!"

The earth was falling quickly now, and soon they were buried once more, but with far less space above them.

"A little further," Seph cried, digging for as long as she could, until she no longer had the energy. "We were so close. So close." She broke down and sobbed.

It was dark now, and quiet apart from the sound of heavy breathing. As his head spun in the breathless stuffiness, something scurried over his face and nipped his nose.

He knew he was near death because that wasn't the only thing he was hallucinating. He was blinded suddenly. A tiny patch of bright light appeared above his head. It took him a moment, until, with watering eyes, he saw her.

Tulip. Burrowing upwards, breaking through the dirt, through to…

The surface.

"Light!" Frank said. "We're here! The surface is right here!"

Once more, he wriggled himself free. He ripped at the soil above him until he saw it. Blue sky. Using more strength than he thought he had, he pushed himself higher with all his might, pulling himself onto fresh green grass.

He reached down and yanked Nora up beside him. Together, they helped everyone else emerge, as they scrunched their eyes shut, not yet ready for a light brighter than any they had known.

They had surfaced in a field somewhere in the countryside. Signs on the road that ran along the bottom of the field were in English and gave the distance to London, a few hundred miles away. Frank was glad to be home.

They sat together on the grass, the eyes of the LSR gradually opening, like babies seeing for the first time. As Cragor ran his fingers through the bright green grass, stunned, Tulip crawled up his arm and returned to his shoulder.

"Good girl," Cragor said, stroking her. "My clever girl."

Seph was the first of them to stand. She wore her sunglasses, her eyes too sensitive to see without them, but she took off her jacket and opened her arms as she let the sunshine warm her skin.

"It's kind of terrifying," Seph said when Frank joined her. She blinked at the sun, almost risen to its peak. It was late morning and a fine day. "But beautiful too. What's that, that second blue glinting on the horizon?"

"The sea," Frank said. "The sparkling sea."

The LSR stood staring for a while, fascinated by flowers, birdsong, the gentle wind. Sunlight.

Cragor crouched and examined a patch of pink and red. "Are these…"

"Tulips," Nora smiled.

With no particular final destination in mind and no particular time they needed to get there, they all ambled together, in shared wonder, towards the sea.

Frank watched them from a distance as they ran like children through the surf, Nora at his side, her hair shining as it moved in the breeze.

Seph and Cragor walked and held hands, pausing only to kiss and hold one another.

He didn't want to tell them yet. They deserved a few moments more. But he saw Seph's face fall as she noticed.

Frank had spotted them a few minutes before. The beach ended several hundred metres away, where it met the side of a cliff. It had a small cave where the outer edge of it touched the sea. He thought they were swimmers around the rocks at

THOSE OF THE LIGHT

first, but as they came closer along the beach, he saw her.

Queen Gaeatrix approached, surrounded by a troop of soldiers with large pulse guns in their hands.

Members of the LSR screamed, ran, but Seph paused them with a gesture. She put a hand on Cragor's chest, whispered something, then walked up to face her mother alone.

They talked for quite some time. Frank held Nora, kissed her, stole every moment he could, sure they would be parted, taken by the darkness once more.

To everyone's surprise, Gaeatrix and her men walked back to the cave as Seph returned.

"What happened?" Nora asked, eyes wide with concern, as Cragor and Rockford joined them.

"My mother and I have reached an agreement. She will allow the LSR, as well as you two, to remain above the surface."

"That's amazing!" Frank said. "How did you convince her?"

Seph was stony and expressionless. "I'm to return immediately to marry King Gehen. Now my brother is dead, my mother's position is weak without his alliance. It is the only way she will show mercy to Cragor and allow everyone but me to remain above."

Cragor's face contorted with despair and confusion. "What are you saying? You can't do that. Not after everything. And what about us? I don't want this without you."

"There can still be an us. King Gehen has agreed to allow me to return to the surface, for every half year. My mother has explained what she called my *rebellious nature* and concessions have been made if I am willing to be subdued and accept that King Gehen will take additional wives."

"Jesus, so your mother's selling you into a harem? She's a monster."

"I'll be ok. I'll manage," Seph said, Frank sure she was trying to convince herself more than anyone. "Besides, it'll be six months and then we'll be together for the rest of the year. It will be fine. I'll cope with things below. I'll get used to it. It'll be worth it if we can still have a life."

"Is that what you want?" Cragor said, appalled that Seph—his irrepressible Seph—could accept such a fate. "Half a life? And what about the half a year you spend down there, with a beast in your bed? You can't do that to yourself. I won't let you."

"It's that, or they execute us all."

Cragor and Seph continued to fight as the message spread through the LSR. Everyone protested, but Seph's mind was made up. Cragor stormed off towards the shoreline, kicking the sand with rage.

"This can't be how things end, Seph," Frank said. "What about Cragor and you? He's right. You'll never survive if you're constantly torn between him and Gehen."

Seph sighed. Her whole body sagged, all the fight knocked out of her, her heart already slipping back into the shadows. "Not everyone gets a happy ending, Frank. That's the way the world's always been, whichever part you come from."

Cragor walked with her to the cave a little while later. They deserved their last few minutes together in the sunlight.

When Cragor returned alone, they found shelter in empty beach huts for the night and the next day, Frank and Nora set out to hitchhike to their old house on their own private shore. Cragor, Rockford, Tilourik, and Rillarook came with them. The others left to find their own way in the world, like new conquerors, Seph's gemstones shared out between them.

"We're Londoners," Lillibet said as she left with Rupert. "Always have been, always will be. We're headed back to the east end. I do hope Mrs Sumpkins shop is still in business. I could murder some jellied eels."

Cragor was quiet as they made their way to the beach house. Frank was certain the kids wouldn't have sold it yet and, sure enough, the spare key was where he had always kept it, in a plant pot by the door.

Weeks passed and Cragor said little. He slept and ate, stroked Tulip, and would walk along the shore in the black of night. Frank knew he thought of Seph in the darkness.

Frank was as in love with Nora as he had ever been and, despite his fears for Seph, was happy in a way he never thought he could be again. He couldn't help but think about how he'd lost Nora, then gotten her back, about how his life had ended, then been renewed.

He thought about the last thing Seph said to him and decided he didn't quite agree. Not everyone got a happy ending, true, but if recent events were anything to go by, maybe that meant it wasn't the end. Maybe not for Seph or Cragor either.

Maybe another ending was hidden below. Waiting to step into the light.

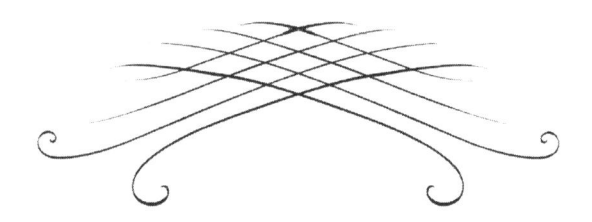

NICOLA CURRIE is a multi-genre writer from Cambridge, England. She writes fiction and poetry for children and adults, and her work can be found in various anthologies and magazines.

A Bath Children's Novel Award longlistee, Nicola lives with her husband, Mark, and their Syrian hamster, Chonka.

NICOLA CURRIE

Bibliography

Bad Romance, Black Hare Press, 2020

Beyond the Realm, Black Hare Press, 2020

Dark Drabbles (*Beyond, Unravel, Apocalypse, Love, Hate, Oceans, Ancients*), Black Hare Press, 2019/2020

Envy, Black Hare Press, 2020

Greed, Black Hare Press, 2020

Lust, Black Hare Press, 2020

Midnight in the Witch's Kitchen, Alban Lake Publishing 2020

Mother Ghost's Grimm Volume 1, NBH Publishing, 2019

Mother Ghost's Grimm Volume 2, Nocturnal Sires Publishing, 2020

Pride, Black Hare Press, 2020

Quietus 13, Black Hare Press, 2020

Sloth, Black Hare Press, 2020

Starlings, Sarasvati Magazine, 2019

The Border Wall, Mslexia Magazine, 2014

The Tides, Sarasvati Magazine, 2019

Timekeeper, Sylvia Magazine, 2021

Twenty Twenty, Black Hare Press, 2020

Vixen, Sarasvati Magazine, 2019

Wrath, Black Hare Press, 2021

Connect

Twitter: @Speculative_Nic

Amazon: amazon.com/Nicola-Currie/e/B07YYHZFKY/5

NICOLA CURRIE

BLACK HARE PRESS is a small, independent publisher based in Melbourne, Australia.

Founded in 2018, our aim has always been to champion emerging authors from all around the globe and offer opportunities for them to participate in speculative fiction and horror short story anthologies.

Connect: linktr.ee/blackharepress

Printed in Great Britain
by Amazon